COUNTDOWN TO
DANGER
CHOOSE YOUR OWN ENDING!

For Danielle, Ruby and Léo

Scholastic Canada Ltd.
604 King Street West, Toronto, Ontario M5V 1E1, Canada

Scholastic Inc.
557 Broadway, New York, NY 10012, USA

Scholastic Australia Pty Limited
PO Box 579, Gosford, NSW 2250, Australia

Scholastic New Zealand Limited
Private Bag 94407, Botany, Manukau 2163, New Zealand

Scholastic Children's Books
Euston House, 24 Eversholt Street, London NW1 1DB, UK

www.scholastic.ca

Library and Archives Canada Cataloguing in Publication
Title: Horror house / Jeff Szpirglas.
Names: Szpirglas, Jeff, author.
Description: Series statement: Countdown to danger: choose your ending!
Identifiers: Canadiana (print) 2021037618X | Canadiana (ebook) 20210376198 |
ISBN 9781443189613 (softcover) | ISBN 9781443189620 (ebook)
Subjects: LCSH: Plot-your-own stories. | LCGFT: Choose-your-own stories.
Classification: LCC PS8637.Z65 H67 2022 | DDC jC813/.6—dc23

Photos ©: cover timer and throughout: milmirko/Getty Images; clock throughout: Samarskaya/Getty Images.
All other photos © Shutterstock.com.

7 6 5 4 3 2 1   Printed in Canada 114   22 23 24 25 26

MIX
Paper from
responsible sources
FSC® C016245

JEFF SZPIRGLAS

COUNTDOWN TO DANGER

CHOOSE YOUR OWN ENDING!

HORROR HOUSE

Scholastic Canada Ltd.
Toronto New York London Auckland Sydney
Mexico City New Delhi Hong Kong Buenos Aires

30:00

The door slams behind you. You turn around and grasp the handle. It should open, but it doesn't. "Kanisha?" you say nervously, and turn back to face the inside of the old, abandoned house you entered only moments ago.

Your cousin is here on a mission, already holding her video camera in one hand. In her pocket is a device she claims can detect the "essence" of "spectral entities." You're not entirely sure you buy that, but this place definitely gives you the creeps.

"The door won't open," you tell her. "What if this place is, like, *really* haunted?"

"Good," Kanisha says. "That's why we came here—to prove it once and for all."

You shake your head. While Kanisha has been busy posting videos about ghosts on her YouTube channel, you've been digging for information at the library.

What was in that old local history book you found there? That this is the house of Avonlea and Abraham Smithson—and it's rumoured to be a gateway to supernatural realms.

You look back at the front door, hoping maybe it was just the wind that snapped it shut, and then you see it.

BLOOD RED LETTERS BEING SCRATCHED INTO THE WOOD.

AT MIDNIGHT YOU ARE OURS.

You let out a yell. Kanisha turns around. "What are you screaming at?"

"Don't you see it?" You point to the door, and sure enough, the writing has vanished. But it was *there.* You pull out your phone to check the time, noticing you have no signal. It's only thirty minutes, you realize, until midnight.

Kanisha steps farther into the house, close to a towering, dusty bookcase. Past it there's a stairwell going up, and one going down. "I'm getting a strong reading from the basement," she says. "Let's try there."

"Don't do it," you plead. "We're in danger." But off she goes. You turn back to try the door again.

YOU CAN'T SAVE HER. WE WILL POSSESS YOU. WE WILL BE FREE!

Yikes! You should get Kanisha and get out of here. But then a flutter of movement down the hall catches your attention. Maybe it's just the wind. Maybe it's . . . you gulp . . . a ghost?

If you go down to the basement to look for Kanisha, turn to page 39.
If you explore the main-floor hallway, turn to page 55.

12:53

You look at the fireplace and hold your breath. The intense heat sizzles your skin, but you step forward anyway, ducking to keep from bonking your head on the stone mantel. You are engulfed by the searing flames, and you open your mouth to scream in agony when—

Darkness.

The flames vanish. The pain immediately ceases.

You rub your arms and legs just to make sure they're still there.

You take a tentative step forward. Your foot touches something cold and wet. Something that definitely hasn't been roasted.

Another step, and this time there's a squelch as your foot sinks into muck. White smoke wafts into view, and you try to wave it off. The smoke swirls with the movement of your hand. You get a whiff of it, and—it's not smoke. It has the earthy smell of a fog, or a mist.

You take a few more steps, and the world around you opens up. Through the thick fog, you spot several dark shapes that are waist high and still as the dead.

They're still as the dead because they're tombstones.

You're standing in the middle of the graveyard. It's

dark, but the full moon above casts a useful glow over the place.

You whip around to look for any sign of the fireplace, but it has either a) completely vanished, or b) been obscured by the thick fog. Regardless, you can worry about how you are going to get back into Smithson House later.

You don't have much time, and if Smithson is right, you have to retrieve the page by digging up her grave. You hope there's a shovel or something around here. Plus, you still need to find her grave.

On the other hand, now you're outside. You could just run out of here and find someone to help rescue Kanisha.

If you look for the grave, turn to page 76.

If you leave, turn to page 59.

19:05

You hurl the knife at the painting. At the very least, it makes a cool *SHHH-DOINK!* noise as the blade slams into the canvas.

It's lodged right in the middle of the woman. You can't believe it—she's still just a painting, but now she's standing there inside the canvas, writhing back and forth.

She looks down at the knife and laughs. "Nice try!"

Breathing heavily, you watch the woman push at the knife.

A second later, the metal blade clatters to the floor.

With one hand clutching her belly, the woman slowly looks up at you. "That was a mistake."

The entire painting, even the frame, begins to vibrate. A low noise fills the basement, making your ears tremble, and you watch as the woman reaches out, her hand passing beyond the canvas and into the real world. Her arm takes on three-dimensional form, but her skin still looks like it's been finished with brush strokes. She grabs hold of the frame and pulls hard. Her knee juts out of the canvas.

"Don't think you can escape," she says.

You stare, dumbfounded, as the woman pulls

herself further and further out of the painting. Who knows what she's capable of in the real world?

You look around. The knife is useless. Clearly you can't stop a painting with a knife.

But you realize there's paint leaking out of her "wound." Not blood. Paint.

You back up, searching the room for anything you can use to slow her down, and see a shelf full of paint cans on the far wall. That's it! You can "erase" her by painting over her.

"No!" she screams.

You rush over to the shelf, throwing down several cans. They land with hollow thuds. Empty!

Now it's your turn to scream, "No!"

You whip your head around. The woman is nearly out of the painting. Her feverish, furious eyes are locked on you.

You fumble through the shelf, picking up can after can, shaking them. Some have liquid inside, but not enough.

She's out of the painting now and walking towards you. She's not fast but she's closing in, and she's put herself between you and the stairway to the main floor.

As you search, you hear a metallic sound behind you, and you turn to see her standing there—HOLDING THE KNIFE!

Without thinking, you pick up one of the empty

cans and hurl it at her. The can smacks against her face with a loud clang. She winces and shakes her head. "That won't work," she says.

You eye the knife in her hand and throw another can, this time right at her arm.

You turn, looking for more cans, and now you see a jar with liquid in it and *PAINT THINNER* written on its side. You take a running dive at it and start to loosen the lid.

The woman's right on your tail. Her icy hands sink into your back. Searing pain flares from where she's gripping you.

"I've got you now," she hisses.

THE PAIN! You drop to your knees. You can feel her breath on your back. It smells of paint. Her wound is dripping more paint onto you. You grit your teeth, turn around, and fling the jar right at her.

Turn to page 61.

01:07

"**T**hree!"

Kanisha's fingers poke out into a pair of scissors.

"Yes!" you say. You bump her fingers and step back. Kanisha looks like she can't believe what just happened.

"The house is yours," says the ghost closest to you. "And us with it. Unless you choose to set us free . . ."

"You should keep them here," Kanisha says. "Think of the power you would wield."

You turn from Kanisha to the ghosts. Their sunken eyes and sullen faces fill you with remorse. You shake your head. "You guys want your freedom? You got it."

You blink, and they are gone. The house is empty except for you and Kanisha.

"I hope you're happy," she says. "Now that you've freed the spirits, how am I going to film *Haunts and Homes*?"

You look around at the decrepit old house that is now yours. You step on a creaky floorboard, and an idea hits you. "What about a home renovation show instead? This place is *dying* for a makeover."

00:00

You survived! There are ten other ways to escape the danger—try to find them all!

5256031700

You look from Smithson to the pages spread across the table. "Wait, what are you writing?" you ask. You step closer to her and see that it's not a diary or novel or anything like that. The words don't even make sense.

"Incantations," she says, gesturing at the old, battered books piled on the table. They must be ancient. You spot the words "mystic" and "spells" along some of their crumbling spines.

"I have been doing research," she says. "I believe that with the right combination of spells, I can communicate with spirits from beyond our astral plane. I am in the process of compiling everything into a book."

"Yeah," you say. "I think you might be on the right track."

Then you realize—this book must be what conjured the ghosts who trapped you here. And if she doesn't finish writing the book, the spirits won't end up in the house.

You need to stop her from writing. But how?

If you tell her you're from the future, turn to page 119.
If you take the papers from her, turn to page 85.

24:48

You'd better not mess around with the clock *too* much. You get on your tiptoes and turn the big hand counter-clockwise, then step back.

Tick. Tick. Tick. It's still working.

You hear a noise in the hall, so you march back to the main foyer. There's Kanisha! She's standing there with her flashlight, her camcorder and—

And you! Standing where you actually were five minutes ago. Five minutes, you realize, is how far you turned the clock back.

"WHAT THE HECK?!" you shout. Only it's not you shouting, it's Other You.

Kanisha turns from Now You to Other You and shakes her head. She holds up the camera. "I don't know what's going on, but it's gonna be on *Haunts and Homes*!" she says. You're not sure which You she's talking to.

You double back to the clock room with Kanisha running after you. You skid to a halt in front of the clock. Kanisha is recording everything, but keeping her distance.

You peer at the clock, trying to think . . .

If you turn the hands forward, turn to page 74.
If you turn the hands back even more, turn to page 70.

10:28

You're not digging anything up until you know for certain you've found the right grave.

You stroll through the tombstones, eyes cast on their weathered surfaces. You must be staring at them pretty intently because you completely miss the OTHER PERSON in the graveyard until you bump right into him.

Both of you tumble to the ground. You get up quickly, scrambling for your shovel to defend yourself. But the man has already gotten to his feet and is looking you over. He's dressed in an old-fashioned suit, and his skin is pale and clammy.

"I can help you," he says, holding out his hand. His voice is weirdly out of sync with his movements, like they haven't quite caught up. Plus, his face is kind of familiar. What's the deal with this guy?

Then it hits you. You recognize him from your library book. "You're Abraham Smithson," you say.

The man gives a polite nod.

"You're dead," you say, matter-of-factly.

"I was dead. I suppose I still am. Mostly."

"Mostly?"

"Things from my home never quite . . . die. They

linger. The house, you see, is built on a soft spot between the living world and the world beyond. And this grave-yard sits on another plane of reality, poised between the living and the dead."

"Well, I'd like to get back to my own reality."

Abraham nods. "That's a tricky one. I take it you've come through the fireplace."

"Yeah, your wife sent me here. Well, her ghost did, I guess. But why's she in that bricked-up room? Totally weird, man."

Abraham's face goes pale. And that's saying some-thing since he's already mostly dead.

"She wanted the missing page of that book. You know where her grave is, by any chance?"

"Avonlea is *not* in that room," he says icily.

"Sure she is."

Abraham shakes his head vigorously. "It looks like her. It talks like her. But it isn't her."

You hear low, squelchy sounds coming from the mist. Like something big is approaching.

You narrow your eyes. "What do you mean IT?"

"It must have followed you here," Abraham says. "This is a trap, no doubt. You need to come with me. I know how to stop it."

If you follow Abraham, turn to page 46.

If you stand your ground, turn to page 102.

10:40

"Just turn the mirror so I can get a better look."

"I dunno," Kanisha says. "It's like finding a needle in a haystack."

"Just do it," you say. "And be careful."

"Okay, okay," Kanisha retorts. She grabs the mirror and pulls it towards her. But she stumbles under your weight, then the ground rushes up to you, and . . .

SMASH!

Kanisha reappears with a sheepish look on her face. "Whoops. Are you okay?"

"Am I okay? I'm in bits and pieces!"

"No, your reflection is just in this one piece. Weird."

You roll your eyes. "Well, pick me up then."

She digs into her pocket and pulls out some old tissues. Using the tissues, she grabs your shard of mirror. Your whole body lifts away from the ground as you stare into Kanisha's large face. You must be a tiny fragment of yourself. This isn't good. How are you going to get out of here now? That book is going to be so hard to find in the attic. You wish there was a bookshelf like the one downstairs, and—

"Kanisha! I think I know where the book is!"

Turn to page 127.

18:49

You can tell she is studying your face as you process what she's just told you. "How do I know I can trust you?" you ask.

"You don't."

"That's not helpful!"

You wish Kanisha were here, but the ghosts probably got to her already. And that's the thing—not only do you have to stop the ghosts, but you've got to find your cousin. You should at least hear Smithson out. "What do I have to do?"

Avonlea Smithson puts her hands on the sides of the frame and leans forward. You get the feeling she would lean right out of the painting if she could, because her face comes up to the canvas but she can't push past it. "It's because of my book of spells," she begins, and you shiver. "The spells and incantations in its pages can summon spirits. Evil spirits. They're the ones trying to break into your world. It looks like they're finally going to do just that, and then you'll be dead and I'll be stuck in this painting forever. But if you find my book and reverse the spell, you can stop them."

"How do I reverse the spell? And what spell?"

"That's easy. *Incantus Iniquitous*. You have to read it backwards."

"Okay," you say, thinking this through. "I can do that, I think. I just need to find the right page of the right book. What's it called?"

Smithson sighs. "Unfortunately, it was not labelled."

"Great," you mutter. "What colour is it?"

"I seem to remember it being a leather-bound book."

You shake your hands at the painting. "But this house has a ton of leather-bound books."

"You're right. I wish you luck in finding the correct one."

Hang on a second. What if Avonlea Smithson *is* one of the ghosts that is trying to possess you and break into the human world? What if this is all a horrible scheme to send you on a wild goose chase?

If you ignore her instructions, turn to page 49.

If you try looking for the book, turn to page 123.

02:29

You pick up the book. You've never seen this language before, so the spell looks like a bunch of gobbledygook. Maybe this wasn't a good idea. Maybe you should have gone after Kanisha. You call her name, but now you can't hear anything except the echo of your own voice. You'll have to try reading this.

"Tsoh ruoy nruter ot sdrawkcab ti yas stsohg eht hsaelnu ot drawrof ti kaeps."

You're about to throw the book down in a fit of frustration when you remember what Smithson told you.

You've got to read it *backwards*.

You stare at the words a moment longer. Your eyes narrow as you start to decode what's written there. "Hang on a second," you say. Slowly, you speak the words.

"Speak it forward to unleash the ghosts," you say.

Piercing cries ring out. The whispers calling your name are louder now. They're coming from all directions. You clamp your hands over your ears, but the voices push their way into your mind. They're yelling at you.

And you can hear Kanisha's voice, screaming in agony.

"Speak it forward to unleash the ghosts," you say again, trying to make yourself heard over the din. A wind whips up and you have to press your hands on the book to keep the pages open. Screaming from invisible ghosts fills your mind as you try to say the words one more time. "SPEAK IT FORWARD TO UNLEASH THE GHOSTS, SAY IT BACKWARDS TO RETURN YOUR HOST!"

Silence.

The wind dies. The voices stop. You take a shaky breath. You don't close the book—not yet.

You stare around the room. Slowly, your eyes are adjusting to being in here. You wonder if they would have done so sooner had it not been for the ghosts.

It's just a barren old room. It seems smaller than it did when you first entered—not much bigger than a closet, really. Only there's no Kanisha. Where is she?

A hand clamps down on your shoulder. You jump.

"There you are!" she says.

You turn, and sure enough, Kanisha is now standing in front of you. Behind her, you see the half-open bookcase.

She doesn't seem scared or anything. She's got her camera in one hand, and the recording light is on.

You open your mouth, but words don't come out.

"I was wondering where you were," she says.

"You mean, you weren't in here with me?"

She looks at you and shrugs. "I've been searching this place for something cool. Looks like you found a hidden room. Nice one!"

You shake your head. "Have you not heard me running around this house calling you?"

"What can I say? Sometimes when I'm on camera, I get a bit laser focused." She looks past you. "Hey, what's that old book? It looks important."

She starts to walk towards it, but you put your hand out to stop her. "No way, Kanisha. Don't touch it."

She gives you a sideways glance. "What's in that book?" she asks.

You smile. "Just some old gobbledygook."

You hear the clock in the main hall begin to chime midnight. You want to take Kanisha down to the basement and show her Avonlea Smithson, but you suspect she's nothing more than a painting now . . .

00:00

You survived! There are ten other ways to escape the danger—try to find them all!

24:48

Thump!

You fall back and your head knocks against the floorboards. Ouch! Floorboards are HARD.

Slowly, painfully, you pull yourself up. You rub the back of your head with one hand. The other is still clutching the pages you grabbed from Avonlea.

A hand reaches out to pull you to your feet. "Thanks, Kanisha," you say. Only it isn't Kanisha.

It's Avonlea Smithson.

You blink. She's looking in your direction, but her gaze goes past you.

You're trying to make sense of this. "Hang on a second. You're not supposed to be here."

"What . . . has . . . happened?" Avonlea asks in a daze.

You hear footsteps. Both of you turn to see Kanisha running into the room. She skids to a halt and points.

"Who is THAT?" she asks, kind of rudely.

But Smithson is busy looking around the room. For you, it's back to the way it was. For her, her house has suddenly become an old, abandoned dump full of cobwebs—and ghosts.

"Oh, this is Avonlea Smithson."

"Who?"

"Smithson. It's her house, Kanisha." You think about this. "*Was* her house. This time-travel stuff is weird." You turn to Smithson. "Welcome to the future," you tell her. You look down at the papers in your hand.

"What's that?" Kanisha asks.

"These," you say, "will become the book that summons the ghosts."

Kanisha narrows her eyes. "What ghosts?"

"Duh, the ones you wanted to put on your YouTube channel. You can't have *Haunts and Homes* without haunts, right?"

Kanisha shrugs and motions to the old house. "You know *Rock the Wreck* is the name of my home renovation channel."

Now it's your turn to look as confused as Avonlea, who's wandering around brushing dust off shelves and cobwebs from pictures.

Then it hits you. "I did it! I took the book, so Smithson never used it. She never summoned any spirits. This house never got haunted."

You've changed history.

You think about this. You must have gone back pretty far in time. It's wild how changing one little thing like Avonlea and her book has affected the present. Kanisha's YouTube videos aren't about haunted houses anymore.

You make your way to the front door, then pull it

open and step outside. That's when you stop. And you stare.

"That's impossible," you gasp.

You're not staring at the cars. Or the houses. Or even the owls in the trees. (Yes, there are lots of owls.)

No, you're staring at the people WALKING THEIR PET RHINOCEROSES up and down the block.

"What's wrong?" Kanisha asks.

You point to the rhinos. "What are they doing here?"

Kanisha laughs. "If you don't walk your rhino, they go to the bathroom all over the house. You of all people should know that."

You turn to her. "What are you talking about?"

"Uh, didn't you take Floyd for a walk before coming here?"

You very slowly shake your head.

"Then we'd better get back before he gouges another hole in the wall," she says. Kanisha pulls you out of the house. You leave Avonlea Smithson there; you'll be back soon enough to sort that out. First you've got to get home and see what Floyd has been up to.

Hey, at least rhinoceroses don't seem to be on the endangered species list anymore . . .

00:00

You survived! There are ten other ways to escape the danger—try to find them all!

01:07

"Three!"

You watch as Kanisha's fingers curl into a fist. "No!" you blurt. A crooked smile peels across her lips.

"Well, I guess that's game," you say.

She shakes her head. "Not quite. Remember what I said about the house consuming the loser?"

You don't get it. Not at first. You try to take a step, but your foot won't move. You look down.

It's stuck to the floor.

No, not stuck. The creaky floorboards are overlapping your feet. You try to pull yourself out of the tangled mess covering your ankles, but you lose your balance. You topple forward and SMASH face first onto the floor.

Instantly the floor pushes into your chest and legs and throat. You feel your body lengthen and thin out, transforming from flesh and blood into board and nail.

You look up to see Kanisha walking towards you. Walking ON you.

You hear her feet squeak against the floorboards.

And then you hear nothing at all.

THE END.
To try again, go back to page 24.

22:26

You're shocked to discover an entire room behind the wall. How is that even possible? You can't make out any actual entrance to it, but you spot light coming from a fireplace at the far end and bookcases lining the walls—

You stop in your tracks. Someone with long, dark hair is rocking back and forth in a chair by the fireplace. She's facing away from you, but you're sure of who it is.

"Kanisha?" you whisper. Your cousin keeps rocking.

"I'm coming," you say. You smash the frying pan against the wall over and over. Plaster rains down. You make a hole big enough to squeeze through.

You take a few steps forward and feel the fire's heat.

"Kanisha?"

She turns around, and your heart catches in your throat. It's not your cousin, but a woman with harsh, piercing eyes. "Why have you disturbed my slumber?"

"Uhhh . . ." you start. "I'm sorry. I can fix the wall. I thought you were stuck in here, and—"

"My name is Avonlea Smithson. And *you* are trespassing in my home!"

"Avonlea Smithson?!" you say. You can feel your stomach knotting. "You're a gh—"

Turn to page 112.

15:27

You're not sure how long you've been in mid-air before you wonder a) whether you'll ever hit the bottom, and b) if you do, how badly your body will be broken—

SPLASH!

You choke back water and paddle madly to the surface. Is there some kind of river below the house? How can that be? You look around. Up ahead, the river widens. In the distance, there's a lone boat. A cloaked figure stands at the bow, pushing it along with a stick. But you don't have any more time to get your bearings because suddenly you're being carried by a swift current.

You try to stay afloat, but the water is moving too fast.

"Help!" you gurgle, but you're pretty sure you can't be heard over the rushing water.

There are riverbanks on either side, bordered by rocky walls that stretch up into the darkness.

The river pushes your farther, faster. The boat looms into view. You get an uneasy feeling about the boatman, but the riverbank is your only other option.

If you swim to the boat, turn to page 91.

If you swim to the riverbank, turn to page 57.

07:55

You've seen enough living dead movies to know that while zombies may dine on human flesh, they are slow. "Catch you later, dude!" you shout at the zombie. You even manage to give a teasing wave before you turn and get back to running around the tombstones.

As long as you keep your eyes peeled for any other signs of danger, you'll be able to outrun this creature long enough to find the gate, get out of here, and get help.

WHUMP!

You trip over a tree root and fall face first into yet another patch of mud.

"Gahhh!" you shout. How much mud can you fall into in one day? And why are there so many tree roots in this graveyard?

You try to get up but your foot is caught between the root and the ground. It's really twisted in there. You reach forward to pull it out.

No good.

In the distance, the squelchy sounds of the zombie lumber slowly, steadily towards you. A minute later its silhouette appears through the mist.

"Oh no."

You can still do this. You just need to pull on the root and create a little extra space to loosen your foot. But it won't budge. Now your hands are slippery from all the mud.

You fumble through your pockets. There's got to be something you can use to cut through the root. Maybe a set of keys?

You fish out your house key and start sawing through the root. Back and forth, back and forth. Yes! You're making progress. You've cut a small notch in it already. If you can just keep going long enough to weaken it so you can break through—

"Urrrghghrghhrghrrr," a voice calls from above you.

You look up.

The zombie towers over you. A splash of cold saliva lands on your hand. The zombie bends down so that it's kneeling over you. Its eyes seem to roll in their sockets. It opens its mouth and lets out a deathly burp.

Then the zombie takes hold of your leg once again. It bends forward and opens its mouth.

Dinnertime!

THE END.

To try again, go back to page 59.

03:19

"Hey, Mrs. Smithson," you say. "How did you escape from that painting? I'm all ears."

"I wasn't trapped in that painting, child. I put myself there, and I deliberately placed the mirror beside it," she says, moving closer to you. You keep your eyes locked on Smithson and hope it gives Kanisha the edge she needs.

"I lay in wait," Smithson continues. "One by one they came. Some seeking treasure, some fortune. Some by mere chance." Smithson points to the ghosts in the mirror with you. "Eventually they found their way down to me, like prey to a spider. *You* were easy, child. You stumbled and fell into my trap like the fool you are. And now there is no escape!"

"Yeah, but why?"

"Because I never truly died. I exist in a state between life and death. Every living soul I trap gives me strength, and as you fade into the ether of the after-life, I will become living once again!"

You see Kanisha moving in your peripheral vision. She's found something. You keep stalling. "But I'm not dead." You think about this. "Am I?"

"You soon will be! And nothing can stop me."

"Except that book of spells," you muse.

Smithson grins. "You will not find it. You would not be able to use it if you did."

"Do you mean *this* book of spells?" Kanisha says, holding up an old, weathered book.

Smithson's eyes go wide. "GIVE THAT TO ME!" she screams.

"Nuh-uh," Kanisha says, whipping the book behind her.

"She found the book!" exclaims the eyeless ghost.

"She must read . . . the ninth page," another chimes in. "Third paragraph."

It's like they've tried this before. Tried and failed, mind you.

"Backwards," says the eyeless ghost. "But she cannot make a mistake. Reading it incorrectly is bad for one's vision."

Kanisha jumps onto a table to avoid Smithson.

"She's just a ghost," you say. "She can't physically harm you, right?"

Smithson SMASHES the table into pieces. Bits of it bounce off the mirror.

"I guess she can." You call Kanisha over. "Quick, bring the book here."

She dodges Smithson and rushes up to the mirror. "What do I do?"

If you tell her to read the incantation, turn to page 53.
If you read it yourself, turn to page 62.

06:44

You can't reach the top shelf on your own, and there's no time to waste. Why not at least start with *Tobin's Spirit Guide* and see where that takes you? You blow a puff of air at the shelf to clear the cobwebs, but all you get is a face full of dust.

You cough and wipe the brown sediment off your face. Gross!

Then you swipe away the layer of sticky cobwebs and push the other books out of the way. The shelf is not packed too tightly, so it should be easy to pull the book out.

You wrap your fingers around the spine and give it a tug, but it doesn't seem to want to come off the shelf.

Huh. Maybe it's caught on something?

You pull harder, and the book barely budges. You keep pulling, tightening your muscles. The book inches out a little. You're consumed with grabbing the book, pulling with all your might, until—

POP!

You go flying backwards, landing on the floor with a thud.

You feel the weight of something on your body. You reach over to pull *Tobin's Spirit Guide* off your chest and stare at it. The book is undamaged. If it wasn't caught on anything, why was it so hard to yank off the shelf?

You get on your hands and knees, and you see it.

A dark, empty space where the book had been.

You stand up, moving closer. Is it just a shadow? A trick of the light? How can there be a void like that on a bookcase?

It's as if there's something beyond the shelf, beyond the wall where the shelf is positioned.

You put *Tobin's Spirit Guide* down and pick up the lantern. You stand right in front of the hole. It's a small, vacant spot between the books. You hold the lantern right up to it, hoping to reveal a wall or something solid, but the light is swallowed by black emptiness.

You decide to see how deep it goes.

There's no stick or broom lying in reach, so you decide to test it with your arm. Maybe the real book of incantations is in this little void, waiting for you!

Slowly, cautiously, you reach your hand in. Your fingers stretch, groping into the darkness . . .

SOMETHING CLAMPS DOWN ON YOUR WRIST. HARD!

You scream.

Instinctively, you try to pull your arm out. For a second, you get the upper hand. Your wrist and hand emerge back into the light—

Another hand is clamped around your own. And it's NOT a regular hand . . .

This one's larger, bulkier . . . HAIRIER! Its skin is covered with boils leaking slime right onto you. Its fingernails are red and long and sharp. They dig into your flesh, and you scream again.

But the sound is torn from your lungs as the hand pulls you back in. Pulls your whole arm into the little hole in the bookshelf.

Is it going to pull your arm off?

No, you keep moving forward. You feel the books tumble off the shelf as you connect with it. You feel the space widening. You still can't see anything inside the dark realm, but you feel the hand squeezing you tighter, pulling you farther and farther from the human world, into another . . .

THE END.

To try again, go back to page 14.

10:40

You wait as Kanisha rummages around the attic. She opens old boxes and spills out the contents. She goes through shelves. "There's nothing," she says finally. "We're just wasting time."

Then a voice from behind you moans, "You MUST find that book . . ."

You let out a scream.

"What's happening?" Kanisha says.

You point to the mirror behind you. It's reflecting the space where Kanisha is standing—except now she's surrounded by several ghosts. They're wearing old-timey clothes and their faces are gaunt and pale. One of them is missing its eyeballs. Gross!

Kanisha whirls around with her video camera, looking confused. She's clearly not seeing what you are.

One of the ghosts drifts your way. "Your friend cannot see us. We are here, in the mirror, with you." But it's the next sentence that makes you gulp.

"We have been *waiting* for you."

If you talk to the ghosts, turn to page 86.
If you ignore them, turn to page 121.

07:55

You can run, but you can't hide. You decide you're not going down without a fight. You've never fought a zombie before, but as long as it doesn't bite you, you're set. You look around for a weapon. There's nothing, unless you count those rocks on the ground.

You pick one up and hurl it at the zombie. It bounces harmlessly off its chest.

"Nope," you say. "That's not going to work."

"Urrrghrghrhghrrr," the zombie says.

"Yeah, I got it," you tell it. You're not sure why it's even worth engaging with this undead monster, but the humour makes you feel less afraid of your possible impending doom.

The zombie lumbers over and takes a swipe at you.

It's a zombie, after all, so the punch isn't terribly strong or terribly fast.

You duck.

The zombie hits nothing but air and topples forward, right into one of the tombstones. *Bonk!*

"Nice try!" you say, skipping out of the way as the zombie staggers about in a daze.

It rubs its head and then lets out an annoyed "Urgghrhghrghr!"

"Well, don't try eating me, then!" you say, ready to avoid getting bitten or punched a second time. "I'm just trying to get out of this place."

The zombie stops and stares at you. It shrugs its shoulders. "RRRRGhrrhgurgh?" it says, like it's asking you a question.

"What?"

This time the zombie points at you. It doesn't move forward. "Urghrhrhghr!"

You realize it's not trying to bite or hit you. You have a funny feeling it's actually trying to TALK to you.

The zombie waves you over. At least, that's what you take it to be doing. "Urrghrhg!"

"You want me to follow you?"

The zombie gives a guttural grunt. Amazingly, it moves away from you and farther into the graveyard.

You stand there as mist swirls around the space left by the creature.

"Aw, man," you say aloud. "I'm going to have to follow it, aren't I?"

You don't even bother answering your own silly question. "Wait up!" you say, and run into the darkness.
Turn to page 94.

03:38

You've got this. That axe sliced right through a tombstone, for goodness' sake.

Raising the axe high above your head, you SWING IT DOWN right on the creature's tentacle. You expect it to come clean off, like in the movies. You know, the ones your parents won't let you watch until you're in high school. Good old gore-fests with spurting blood and ear-piercing screams.

What actually happens is the blade BOUNCES OFF the tentacle like it's a piece of rubber. Heck, it even makes a *BOINNNNG!* sound as it flies from your hands and into the mud behind you.

The monster looks down at you.

"Oh no . . ."

Then you see a tentacle coming your way. You've eaten your share of octopus and squid at seafood restaurants, and as the giant tentacle crashes towards you, you realize maybe this is the ocean's form of poetic justice.

And that gore-fest with the ear-piercing screams? Well, let's just say you're on the receiving end of this one.

THE END.

To try again, go back to page 76.

19:05

You roll over, reach back, and hurl the knife towards the painting with all your might. It flies through the air, past the painting, and bounces off one of the shelves. It lands on the bare floor with a useless thud.

"D'oh!" you shout.

You flip back around, looking for something else to throw at the painting, but—

Your chin scrapes against the muddy floor as you're suddenly dragged backwards by your ankle. You turn your head to see the ghostly sheet has wrapped itself tightly around your leg.

The sheet trails all the way back to the painting, and your heart jumps.

The woman in the painting is reaching out her arms and HOLDING THE SHEET.

"No!" you scream, but your cry is cut short as she yanks the sheet towards the canvas. Your face slams against the dirty floor, and you choke on dirt and grime. You reach out, but there's nothing to grab on to.

Your fingernails carve meagre ruts in the ground as you're pulled farther and farther, and now something is gripping your other ankle. It's so icy cold that you can feel it through your clothes.

Suddenly you're hoisted up off the ground and left dangling in the air. You spin around, coming face to face with the horrific image of the woman in the painting. She has a shock of wild black hair. Her skin is bone white, her eyes are bloodshot, and her teeth seem to be lengthening before your very eyes.

"Is that any way to admire my portrait?" she hisses.

"Put me down! I'll help you! I swear it!"

Her grip around your ankles tightens. The woman nods, her eyes rolling in their sockets like marbles. "Oh, you will be a great help. I need someone to hold my place."

She doesn't say any more.

Instead, she gives you a hefty flick, and you find yourself tumbling and turning. You should have hit the ground by now, but you feel a force pulling you back. Your arms and legs don't move the way they once did. They feel . . . flattened, somehow. You try to reach forward, but it's like the entire universe is pressing against you. You can't even draw in a breath.

You see her—the woman in the painting.

Only she's not in the painting. Not anymore. She's standing on the floor of the basement, moving her arms and legs as if she hasn't stretched them in years. After a moment she turns to you and cracks another grin.

You try to move, to run away, but that invisible force is holding you still.

"What do you know," she starts, narrowing her eyes at you. She reaches down and grabs the big sheet off the floor. "You're quite an attractive piece of art, if I do say so myself."

And before you can do anything, the woman throws the sheet over you, blocking your view with the white linen.

You hear her mutter something about "finding the other one," and then her footsteps fade away. Nobody is coming to find you. Not for a long, long time.

THE END.

To try again, go back to page 79.

28:15

You need to find Kanisha. As you step towards the stairwell, your nose is assaulted with a musty smell from the dank basement. "Kanisha . . . ?" you call out. Your voice echoes, suggesting a cavernous space below.

She hasn't been gone long enough to be out of earshot, but there's no response.

You peer down the stairwell. The limited light in this place isn't enough to see much. You pull out your cellphone and turn on the flashlight. It illuminates a couple of old wooden steps and a rickety railing, but even the super-bright light can't pierce the darkness below.

One more time, loudly: "Kanisha!"

And once again, nothing.

Something must have happened to her. You gulp and take a step. Your body weight makes the stairs creak angrily as you gingerly pace downward.

When you get to the bottom, you snap a picture with your phone. The flash goes off, and for a moment you get a better view of the vast subterranean space and . . . GHOSTS!

Your scream echoes around you.

They were white, and covered with sheets, and—

Wait a second. Ghosts don't wear sheets. That's, like, from old cartoons. You shine your phone's light back on them and see they're just objects covered with sheets. They're tall, rectangular and thin, kind of like mirrors or paintings. In fact, there's a mirror propped up right by one of them. Weird.

You tilt your phone and see an old lantern and a book of matches on a table nearby. You work quickly to light the lantern.

Its glow flickers, making the shadows dance as if they're alive and watching you. Swinging the lantern around, you notice something on the dark earthen floor by the far wall. It's a sizeable hole in the ground, and it appears to be freshly dug. It looks like a person could just slip through it. Could Kanisha actually be down there?

You take a step towards the hole, but as you do so, you hear a breathy voice behind you calling your name. You turn around and push the lantern in the direction of the voice. The only thing it illuminates is an object covered in a sheet. It couldn't be coming from that, could it?

If you investigate the hole, turn to page 126.
If you get a better look at the object, turn to page 79.

14:03

You tumble onto a hard surface.

You look up groggily and rub your body. You ache all over. But you can also feel the heat of a fireplace.

"Nice try," a voice behind you says.

You turn to see Avonlea Smithson staring at you disapprovingly. She's still sitting in her chair, right where you left her.

"Oh, hey there."

"You tried to escape."

"No, no, no . . ." You see the look of disbelief on her face. "Well, maybe a little."

"You fool. You're just wasting valuable time. I told you, you must find the page buried with me."

"Yeah, but you had to at least figure I was going to make a break for it."

"We don't have time for diversions! Only you can stop the horrors of this house. Only you!"

Oh, great. Now what?

If you go back through the fireplace, turn to page 3.

If you go to plan B—take her book and run, turn to page 77.

03:38

Hoisting the axe with all of your strength, you stride boldly to the Ghoulite, clear your throat, and try to get its attention. "Yo, Ghoulash-face," you start.

The monster rotates an eye in your direction.

"Suck on THIS!"

You HURL the axe into the air. In your imagination, it sails beautifully, eventually severing the tentacle that's holding the spell.

Instead, it arcs for a moment and then drops to the ground with a useless *thunk*.

"Oh, dang," you say.

"BWAH-HA-HA-HA!" the creature laughs. "DID YOU THINK THAT WOULD HAVE ANY EFFECT ON ME?"

"No, but THIS will," you hear.

Your ploy has allowed Abraham to free an arm. He can't reach the paper, but he is able to punch the monster right in its red eye.

The Ghoulite SCREAMS and pulls a tentacle to its injured eye—the tentacle holding the paper. That's all Abraham needs. He manages to snatch the paper, crumple it into a ball, and toss it down to you.

"Fifth line down. Read it backwards!" he says, just

before the Ghoulite wraps another tentacle around his mouth.

You catch the paper ball, now covered in slime, and open it up. Fifth line down? Backwards?

The spell isn't even in English. How is this going to do anything? Well, it's worth a shot, but you have to be quick. The Ghoulite is now oozing its way towards you.

You read the incantation backwards. It sounds like a bunch of gobbledygook. There's no way this is actually going to work—

"NOOOOOO!!!" the creature roars as it lets go of Abraham. He falls to the ground and rolls out of the way. The creature, meanwhile, flails its tentacles wildly. You have to jump to avoid being flattened by one of them.

You duck behind a tombstone and look over the edge, and now you can tell why the creature is writhing in agony. Bubbles of goo rise and pop all over the Kandarian Ghoulite's body. The stench makes you want to retch, so you turn away and see Abraham behind the next tombstone over. He's plugged his nose.

"What is happening?" you ask.

"The spell. It reverses everything about the Kandarian Ghoulite! Even its body!"

"Reverses?"

"Yes! It's being turned INSIDE OUT!"

You stare in disbelief as the Ghoulite's cries shift to a gurgle. It twitches and finally flops to the ground.

Slowly, you stand. "That was disgusting," you say. "And kind of awesome."

"No," Abraham warns you. "Not yet."

"What are you talking about? That thing's as dead as dead . . ."

Then it EXPLODES. Hunks of stinking monster and slime spatter all over your face. You gag and wipe the goo from your eyes. You are now covered head to toe in monster guts.

"I did try to warn you," Abraham says, finally stepping away from the tombstone.

"So how do I get out of this place?" you ask. "I mean, I don't see a fireplace anywhere."

Abraham points to the massive hole that the Ghoulite emerged from. "That should get us home."

"You're coming? Are you even able to?"

"We've vanquished the evil from my home. I don't know if my body will remain as is, or if I'll finally be released into a more pleasing afterlife. I've been here for well over a hundred years. I'm eager to find out."

And with that, you and Abraham Smithson begin to crawl into the kind of deep, dark hole that adventures are made from.

00:00

You survived! There are ten other ways to escape the danger—try to find them all!

24:48

You get on your tiptoes and CRANK the hands counter-clockwise. You spin them around and around. You hear whirring, grinding gears from within. The ticking speeds up. This clock is super cool!

But it's hard to concentrate on its sounds and sensations. You are overwhelmed with dizziness, like the world around you is blurring. You shake the fogginess from your head and step away from the clock.

You blink. The dust and cobwebs are gone. The chandelier is lit. And seated at the table is a mysterious-looking woman draped in a black shroud-like dress. She's scribbling something on a paper with a feather dipped in ink. Who still does that?

The woman looks up. "Who are you?" she asks suspiciously. You tell her your name, and ask the same of her.

"My name is Avonlea Smithson. What are you doing in my house?"

"Smithson?" you stammer. "*Your* house?" You step back, shaking your head. "That can't be. You're *dead*!"

"Excuse me?!"

But then it hits you: She is dead. Just not yet.

You've travelled back in time!

Turn to page 9.

04:43

You follow Abraham Smithson deeper into the grave-yard. For a sort-of dead guy, he moves at a good clip, and your walk turns into a slight jog to keep up. You weave through the tombstones, skidding to a halt when he suddenly stops.

"What is it?" you ask, panting.

Abraham holds out a hand as if warning you back. He peers around the misty graveyard. You can't see much, save for the dark outlines of the closest tombstones.

Then you hear it. It's that squelchy, muddy sound. Like something moving across the graveyard. Several *somethings*, in fact. The sounds blend together, and your eyes flit over to Abraham, who's still staring into the opaque mist.

You stop and listen. The sound isn't things moving across the earth. No, it's objects moving THROUGH the earth—of roots being torn from the ground. You take a step back.

A muddy hand emerges from behind a grave.

"Look!" you yell, pointing.

But as you try to get Abraham's attention, you see past him to another tombstone, this one also showing signs of movement from beyond.

Amid the squelchy sounds of limbs thrusting out of muddy graves, you hear the moaning. Unhuman wails pierce the stillness. It's not Avonlea at all. The living dead are pulling themselves out and staggering forward. They lumber through the mist towards you. They're sluggish, but they look hungry.

You grab Abraham by his cold, clammy hand and pull. "Let's get out of here before we're surrounded," you say.

He doesn't budge. "It's too late for that."

"Maybe for you, but I'm still alive." You let him go, looking for an opening to sprint away, but something clasps your elbow and locks it into place.

You turn to see that Abraham is the one holding you there.

"What are you doing? These things are after us."

"Not exactly," he says, shaking his head. "They're after YOU."

"What?"

"I'm sorry. I truly am. But it was the only way . . ."

The zombies continue to move your way. There are easily ten of them, and they close in on you, tightening the circle.

"What are you doing? You said you would help!"

"Avonlea created that book of spells to bring me back," Abraham says. "She didn't realize she would call upon other forces, like that infernal THING in the room. It banished me here. That's why Avonlea bricked it up in the first place."

"Abraham, what have you done—?"

He looks at you, eyes pleading. You try to pull away, but his grip tightens. "We made a deal. That shape-shifting ghoul said it would release me and my dearest Avonlea, but we're far too dead for what it truly desires—a living, breathing body."

Oh no. This whole time, Abraham has been leading you into a trap. You shake your head. "You wouldn't . . ."

Abraham lets go just in time for other sets of hands to grab hold of you. Your arms, your legs. Your head.

You're forced to your knees in the cold mud. You smell the rank, fetid breath of the once-human creatures surrounding you. You look up as their misshapen bodies covered with mud and maggots and moss loom closer, until they're pressing against you, pushing you down into the earth itself . . .

THE END.

To try again, go back to page 76.

14:17

You look past the painting of Avonlea Smithson to the stairwell leading back upstairs. Kanisha has got to be someplace else in this house. You need to find her, and you need to get away from this spooky painting. Smithson claims to be trapped, but you trust her about as much as you'd trust your pet cat to water the plants.

You just need some kind of distraction.

You look around, then point to the far corner of the basement. Your eyes go wide. "Whoa, check it out, dude! It's . . . YOUR MOM!"

Smithson's eyes flit in the direction you're pointing (she fell for THAT ONE?), and you make your big escape.

Or, at least, you try to.

Turns out you didn't tie your shoelaces very well.

Normally you'd be fine, but go figure—this is, like, the ONE TIME your untied shoelace does something ridiculous, like get caught underneath a heavy painting. You stumble forward.

Avonlea's portrait is knocked off balance and starts to topple straight towards you.

You throw your hands out to steady the painting and yourself.

Smithson sees what's happening. "You fool! What are you doing?!"

"Trying to keep from tripping . . ."

"No, watch your step! You're going to fall right back into the mirror!"

Mirror? Oh, right! There's a mirror beside the painting. Isn't that like seven years of bad luck if you break it?

You try to step away, but your shoelace is still caught underneath the painting, and you lose whatever balance you managed to find. You pitch straight backwards and brace for the inevitable smash.

But instead of feeling your body connect with glass, you keep stumbling backwards.

You flip around to see the mirror's surface rushing towards you.

You hold your hands out to protect your face, but they don't hit the glass.

They simply pass . . .

RIGHT.

THROUGH.

IT.

Turn to page 99.

01:52

"I've got this," Kanisha says, clamping the book under her arm. She moves away from the bookshelf, towards the front door.

"Whoa, Kanisha. You've got to *read* the book."

She angles the mirror so you're facing one another. "Yeah," Kanisha returns, "but you never said WHERE I had to read it. Let's blow this place."

"No, no, no. I don't think that's a good idea. Everything that's gone wrong has been in this house—"

"Exactly. We've got to get out of here."

She's walking while she's talking. As Kanisha moves forward, you can see the door. It's ajar.

Like an invitation.

Like the ghosts *want* you to leave.

"Stop, Kanisha. This isn't right."

"Later, cuz. Let's boogie."

But as Kanisha crosses the threshold of the open doorway, you hear a loud scream. She skids to a quick halt and you see the ground coming closer.

Your perspective shifts as she drags one hand over to her side. The mirror is tilted down so you can see the book—

It's burst into flames! Smoke puffs, the pages curl,

and in just a few seconds, the book is a pile of cinders on the ground. Kanisha whimpers and rubs her underarm.

"I knew it!" you blurt. "They wouldn't let us leave as easily as that."

Kanisha grabs hold of the mirror, hobbling further away from the house. "That thing burned me!"

She flips the mirror around. You see the front door slam shut of its own accord. Blood red writing appears on it:

THANKS FOR DESTROYING THE BOOK FOR US. TOO BAD ABOUT THE MIRROR THING, HUH?

You hear a deep laugh emanate from the house itself. The last laugh.

"Oh, great," you say. "The book is gone, and I'm still in here."

"Could be worse," Kanisha says.

"What's worse than this?"

"Well, at least we got out of the house. Plus, now you get to be a real-life Mirror, Mirror on the Wall!"

00:00

You survived! There are ten other ways to escape the danger—try to find them all!

01:40

"**Y**ou can do this," you tell Kanisha. "You just need to read the third paragraph on page nine, uh, backwards."

"Okay, here goes nothing," Kanisha says. She begins to read, but a bone-white hand clamps over her mouth, cutting her off. Another hand grabs the book.

"I am so pleased you found my book," Avonlea says. "I knew it was up here. But I needed that other child to fall into my trap in order to gain the corporeal strength to pick it up. I'm almost whole now, you see."

Kanisha struggles as Avonlea pushes her closer and closer to the mirror.

"These words have great power. Take a look for yourself!" And with that, Avonlea holds the book up to Kanisha. Kanisha screams. When Avonlea pulls the book away, you see what has happened.

Kanisha's eyes are missing!

"No, turn her back!" you yell.

But Avonlea just laughs and thumbs through the book. "I've learned so much and it's all here. I learned how an image not only reflects but can absorb, under the right circumstances."

You watch in horror as Avonlea pushes Kanisha's

face to the mirror's surface. Kanisha lets out a shriek as Avonlea pushes against the back of her head, forcing her into the mirror with you and the other ghosts.

Your cousin whirls around, trying to escape, but her hands bounce harmlessly off the surface of the mirror.

In the attic, Avonlea stretches her arms and legs. Her joints creak and pop. "Ahhh," she says. "I feel pain again. Pain is real. I am real. I have not been real in so very long."

"We'll stop you!" you say.

"I don't think so," she replies. "Over the years, I taught myself so many tricks. I've barely had a chance to use them. But I will now. There's so much out there, beyond this house. Enjoy your stay here!"

You watch helplessly as Avonlea trudges out of the attic.

"And now she will unleash her powers on the rest of the world," the eyeless ghost says.

You realize the extent of what that means. You have only one word to express the horror of it all: "Bummer!"

THE END.

To try again, go back to page 99.

28:15

You tell yourself Kanisha can take care of herself, but honestly—you *hate* basements. Even your own basement gives you the creeps, and that's not in a house that leaves messages on the walls.

Plus, what was that fluttering you saw?

You take a few steps into the main hall of the house. Your feet creak on the ancient wooden floorboards. Dust motes swirl in a shaft of light that must be coming from a window in another room.

A window! That's your ticket out of here! You follow the light through an open doorway and give the window a hefty shove.

It does not move.

Then, as if an invisible presence is fogging up the window, you see words appear . . .

NICE TRY.

You gasp and step back, heart hammering in your throat, and—

DONG!

Whirling around, you spot a grandfather clock weirdly positioned against the far wall, behind an old dining-room table. The minute hand is already past the six, slowly creeping its way to midnight.

You wonder how it could possibly still be running with no one here to wind it.

"SHUT UP, CLOCK!" you roar. And then you turn to the window. "YOU SHUT UP TOO!"

The table is covered in a thick layer of dust, and a chandelier hanging above it is so coated in cobwebs it looks like a giant piece of grey cotton candy. But as you step towards the clock, you notice something odd. It's clean—as if it's recently been wiped down.

The glass is so clean you can even see the reflection of the wall directly behind you.

You turn and narrow your eyes. It's a brick wall. There's nothing odd about that, except . . .

Except all the walls you've seen so far in this place have wallpaper—or rather, they *had* wallpaper. Most of it is peeling off, revealing wood and plaster underneath. Plus, there are bricks strewn across the floor, suggesting somebody added this wall after the fact. Maybe in a hurry too, because why just leave the extra bricks?

Everything in this room is so strange, you're not sure what to investigate first.

If you check out the grandfather clock, turn to page 93.

If you take a closer look at the brick wall, turn to page 73.

10:19

Putting all those swim lessons to good use, you paddle madly through the water. But you're fighting a losing battle as the current keeps pulling you farther into the cavern.

You gasp and choke and splash, not sure if you're making any headway, and then you notice the underground river is coming to a bend. It hits you: Instead of swimming, why not just go with the current and aim towards the shore?

You put your hands in front of your head so your body is shaped like a dart, then you kick with your legs. If you can just reach the shallows . . .

WHUMP!

You let out a cry as you slam into a rock. The wind is knocked out of you. In a panic, you push away from the rock only to discover that your feet can touch the bottom.

You rub your aching side and pull yourself to shore. You slip more than once, banging elbows and knees and scraping your limbs against the rocks, which seem more like an enormous set of teeth than randomly scattered boulders.

With a small stream of blood trailing behind you,

you finally drag yourself onto the narrow strip of land that forms the riverbank. After sucking in a few gulps of air, you get onto your knees, then, shakily, to your feet. You press your hands against the cold, wet rock wall and look up. You can't even see the top of the wall. It disappears into the darkness above, like the cave goes up and up forever.

You look back to the river. The boatman is long gone. The only way out of here is to explore this riverbank further.

If you walk to the left, turn to page 131.
If you go to the right, turn to page 88.

11:46

There's got to be a way out of this place. You make sure your shoes are tied, then you run. You manoeuvre around tombstones like you're on the obstacle course in gym class. You hear your feet splashing through the wet mud and your own rapid breathing.

But there are other sounds mixed into the cacophony. You swear there are footsteps—a slow, lurching kind. And a groaning noise. You hope it's just the wind whipping through the trees, but you can't be sure.

You look over your shoulder. Is that a hand creeping over one of the graves?

WHUMP!

You crash into a tombstone and let out a whimper. You've got to get a hold of yourself. You're nearly there. You pull yourself to your feet.

There are a few more rows of graves, and beyond them . . .

An iron fence surrounds the graveyard. "Sweet!" you cry. You run over and grab hold of the heavy metal bars, hoping they're so ancient and rusted they'll just bend under your weight.

Fat chance.

You look up. There's no way you can climb up the

bars on your own. Plus, the top of the fence is festooned with spikes. Maybe if you climbed onto a tombstone you could get enough height to hop over it, but even then you doubt you can do it without accidentally impaling yourself.

Instead, you start to track around the perimeter of the graveyard, hoping to find a gate that opens.

Now you're sure you hear something trudging along. It's moving slowly but steadily. It sounds big too. You're not dealing with a raccoon here.

You notice a tall tree loom into view. It has big enough branches that you could climb them and maybe get over to the other side of the fence. But the tree is a fair distance away from the fence. You'd have to make a pretty big jump. Should you take your chances with the tombstone-to-fence leap instead?

Suddenly there's a grunting, groaning noise behind you. You can't see too far in the fog, but it doesn't sound like a happy camper. You don't have any more time to decide.

If you climb the tree and jump, turn to page 107.
If you hop the fence from a tombstone, turn to page 111.

08:08

SPLASH! Everything freezes. All you can smell is the strong whiff of paint thinner.

Then the woman begins to move her arms and legs. You try to back away, but she's already got her icy hands on you. Or does she?

You hear a soft fizzing sound as her hand collapses onto itself, liquefying before your eyes. Her expression has changed now. Her eyes and nose are running down her face. Her colours are swirling together.

She can only gargle as she sinks to the floor. The thick puddle of painty goop bubbles once, twice, then extinguishes itself with a wisp of smoke.

You stare at your handiwork. So that's how you're going to deal with these ghosts. Then you hear footsteps and whirl around. Where's the paint thinner?

"Easy, it's just me," Kanisha says.

"Where were you? You missed everything!"

She shakes her head, holding up the camera. "I got it all on here. Now, let's go make some serious art!"

00:00

You survived! There are ten other ways to escape the danger—try to find them all!

01:40

"Let me read it," you say. "Turn to page nine."

Kanisha holds up the book. Cripes! How are you going to read this in time? It's hard enough to focus on reading the words forwards. And Smithson is quickly heading your way. "Hold the page still," you tell Kanisha. "It's got to be done backwards."

"Backwards?" Kanisha says. "Hang on. I can see the words backwards in the reflection."

"Oh, nice," you say. You tell her which paragraph to read. "And do it fast, that ghost is . . ."

"ABOUT TO SWALLOW YOUR SOUL!" Smithson roars.

"Yeah, that."

It's a good thing Kanisha is the best reader in her class. She reads the backwards text as fast as humanly possible.

"NOOOO!" screams Avonlea.

Kanisha's eyes go wide as the phantoms emerge from the mirror and into the attic. "Whoa! Ghosts!"

She picks up her video camera and records the ghosts floating around the room. They move past Kanisha and grab hold of Avonlea.

"LET ME GO!"

They drag Avonlea, kicking and screaming and apparently powerless, towards the mirror. They push her inside.

"Hurry!" one of the ghosts tells you. It reaches a hand into the mirror, clasps you by the wrist, and YANKS you out.

Your body pushes against a membrane-like surface, then a cool gust of air fills your lungs as you SLAM against the floorboards of the attic. But it's an earthly, corporeal pain. And that's a good thing.

Kanisha is at your side in a moment. She props you up, but you don't look her way. Your eyes are cast over to the mirror, where the ghost of Avonlea Smithson is feverishly hammering on the surface. She can't break out. She screams and her eyes go wide—wider than human eyes should. The irises are replaced with black orbs, and her hair billows as if caught in a windstorm. Her flesh goes deathly pale, and her arms and hands wither and twist.

Kanisha's holding up the video camera, and her mouth has dropped open.

"LET ME OUT!" the ghost screams, but its voice is now a high-pitched wheeze.

In response, you grab a dusty old sheet that's lying around the attic and throw it over the mirror. Avonlea screams all kinds of obscenities at you from under the sheet, but you turn to face the other ghosts in the room.

"We are free," the eyeless ghost says, and you see that his eyes are returning to his face. He blinks at you and smiles. "Thank you for saving us. At last, we are free!"

You and Kanisha watch as the ghosts slowly fade into the ether, and you're left alone in the attic.

"Whoa, that will make an awesome episode of *Haunts and Homes*," Kanisha says.

You, on the other hand, stare at that old book of incantations on the floor.

It has the power to revive the dead. It has the power to control all kinds of supernatural forces.

You bend down, pick it up, and open the book. You stare at the handwritten text. "I wonder what else this thing does," you say to yourself . . .

00:00

You survived! There are ten other ways to escape the danger—try to find them all!

05:59

"**L**et me do this," you say. You reach down and grab the shovel. It's heavy. Heavy enough to swing and do some damage.

But that's not your goal. You jam the blade deep into the weeds in front of Smithson's tombstone. You dump a thick, heavy clump of dirt on the ground.

The zombie just stares at you, not moving, not saying anything. You don't like it.

You dig the blade into the mud again. You heave, pulling out more of the wet, sloppy earth. Sweat beads on your forehead.

You dig until you've excavated the top layer of dirt from around the grave. How deep is a casket? You don't want to dig for it, let alone open it, but you need that page.

Time ticks away. Eventually your shovel hits something hard. You get on your hands and knees. They're caked with mud, but you don't care. You feel around for the coffin.

The wood is old and almost soft to the touch. It's decomposing rapidly. That should make it easy to dig through. Heck, you might even be able to pry it open now. You reach for the shovel, but you can't find it.

Oh, there it is. The zombie is holding it. "Hey, give that here!" you say.

"Urrghrhrhgh," says the zombie.

"Yeah, yeah. You're welcome for me doing all the hard work!"

SNAP! CRACK!

You turn just in time to see TWO HANDS explode out of the coffin. The skin around them is withered and blackened. They GRAB HOLD of your shoulders!

The breath is torn from your lungs as you're pulled towards the coffin.

You slam against the exposed wood. You try to squirm out of the way, but the hands' grip is too tight.

"Help!" you manage. You turn your head towards the zombie. "Help me! Please!"

The zombie just grunts. Then it digs the shovel into the pile of earth. It takes a scoop and dumps it on you.

"No!" you manage. Another clump of cold, wet earth splats on your back.

"JOIN US," the thing in the coffin says. Is it Smithson herself? Or has something taken possession of her corpse?

More and more dirt covers your legs, your back, your arms . . . your head . . .

THE END.

To try again, go back to page 59.

06:44

You thrust your arm towards the suspicious-looking book on the top shelf. Sure enough, you can't reach it. The only way to get it is to pull yourself up. You step on one shelf and hold another to keep from falling back. Your clothes are immediately coated in cobwebs, and inhaling the thick layer of dust on the shelves makes you sneeze.

Wiping snot from your nose and tears from your eyes, you pull yourself higher and higher. You feel around for the right book. You don't like heights, and you certainly don't like the idea of falling to the floor.

You fumble around, running your fingers along the spines. They're so gross! But then you finally feel the one book that's sticking out.

"Gotcha!" You pinch it with your fingers and pull. The book starts to inch out, then you hear a loud *CLUNK*.

"What the—?"

You tug at the book, but it won't come free. The harder you pull, the more clicking and clunking you hear from the shelf. Then the bookshelf MOVES.

You hear it grinding, and you realize—it's not a bookshelf.

It's a hidden doorway.

"Oh, crud!" You can't just jump down. You're too scared of heights, and you have instinctively clung to the shelf for dear life. Before you can think of a plan, the shelf whirls around and comes to a stop on the other side of the wall.

You're trapped in darkness. For a moment you hold still, your heart thudding wildly. You can't make out anything in this room—not its size, or what's inside.

Then you hear a whisper. A voice, calling your name.

You can't tell if it's coming from farther into the room or right beside you. You have to take a look. Carefully, you clamber back down the bookshelf until you're standing on solid ground. The light on your phone works, even though there's still no signal.

It's weird. The light doesn't penetrate more than a metre in front of you. It's like the dark in this place is more intense than normal darkness. Even the air feels thicker as you breathe.

You step forward, and the whispers flit about the room. You whip your head around, frantically searching for whoever—or whatever—is saying your name.

There's nothing there.

That's when you hear a loud, piercing scream.

"Kanisha!" you say, stomach sinking. You run in the direction of her screams. "Where are you?"

"Here!" she says. But you can't figure out where "here" is. It sounds like she's everywhere.

You take another few steps and then you see a stone pedestal. Sitting on the pedestal is a book.

It's old and leather-bound, and you're certain it's the one Avonlea Smithson has sent you to find.

You walk over and stare at it. You open the cover and see all kinds of handwritten notes.

"Help me!" Kanisha cries. "They've trapped me and brought me here, but I know the way out. I can get us out of here!"

You look up. "This book is supposed to be the way out."

"Forget the book. Come find me. Let's blow this place and get home!"

You look back to the book and turn a page. There it is—*Incantus Iniquitous*. You just need to read it backwards to undo everything. Unless . . . unless you just don't trust Avonlea Smithson.

If you help Kanisha, turn to page 137.

If you read the incantation, turn to page 16.

29:04

"**S**tay where you are—I'll fix this!" you tell Kanisha and Other You, who has appeared in the doorway.

You get on your tiptoes and turn the clock farther back. How much is enough? Ten minutes? Twenty?

"Oh, no, you don't!" Kanisha jumps forward and wraps her fingers tightly around the minute hand.

"Let go!" you tell her.

She pushes you away, and you fall to the floor. "Ooof!"

You sit up to see Kanisha and Other You fiddling with the clock.

"What is this place?" she wonders aloud, then focuses on you down on the floor. "You don't feel like a ghost."

"I'm not a ghost!" you say. You point to your other self. "I'm you! You from, I dunno, five minutes from now."

"Oh," Other You says. "I don't get it."

How can you explain this? "The clock makes you go through time. I think. I went back five minutes."

"And you just moved its hands?" Kanisha says. She's still trying to figure out how it works. "Forwards or backwards?"

"Backwards. Try twenty minutes," you say.

Kanisha turns the clock back. On cue, you hear a loud *BONG!*

"Quick," you say. "Before they're onto us."

"Who?"

"The ghosts!" Other You says. "They want to trap us here."

"But we're already here," Kanisha says.

"They may not know that," you say.

You get up and look around. Sure enough, the window is now open.

You start running out of the room and down the main hall, towards the door. You grasp the handle and give it a twist. "Yes!" you shout, as the door opens.

You hear footsteps behind you—and screams.

You look over your shoulder. There's Kanisha and Other You, running. In the darkness behind them you see sets of glowing red eyes. You hear a deep, resonant growl.

And you feel the door close, as if being pulled by an invisible force.

"No!" You try to pull it back open. Other You and Kanisha rush to join you.

You can feel the tension in your arms. You can't hold on to the door for much longer . . .

But then you feel yourself being pushed through the doorway. It's Other You, shoving you through. You crash to the ground and feel a heavy body thud on top of you, then another.

Slam! The door shuts.

"Urf," you say, as the three of you disentangle from one another. You manage to get to your feet and find yourself staring at yourself in the moonlight.

"Whoa," you say to yourself in unison. "This is weird."

"You're going to make one awesome YouTube video," Kanisha says, camera in hand. "This is better than a haunted house."

"Let's get out of here," you say.

All three of you make your way across the overgrown grass patch in front of the house, and you see—

Other Kanisha and OTHER Other You!

"Riiiight," you say. "We went back twenty minutes."

Other Kanisha and Other Other You see you and stop cold in their tracks.

"So there are three of you now?" Kanisha says.

"Maybe the other versions of us disappear when time catches up?" you say. Only one way to find out . . .

"What are we supposed to do until then?" Kanisha asks.

You shrug. "Dance party with ourselves?" You pull out your phone and cue up your favourite song.

00:00

You survived! There are ten other ways to escape the danger—try to find them all!

26:42

Something's not right about that wall. You walk over to it and touch the bricks. They feel real enough. Then you make a fist and knock on them. Ouch. Yup, they're brick, all right—

KNOCK. KNOCK.

You step away quickly. Did the wall just knock back at you? Unless . . . What if there's someone back there?

"Hello?" There's no response, so you double back into the hall. You can still hear the knocking as you pace down the hallway and into the next room, a dusty, cobwebby kitchen. You enter, heart beating madly in your chest, and approach the rear wall.

KNOCK. KNOCK.

"Is someone in there?" you say.

KNOCK. KNOCK. There's definitely someone behind that wall. Are they trapped? Do they need help?

The wall here is plaster, not brick. It should break more easily. You grab a cast iron frying pan from one of the kitchen shelves. It's heavy, but you grip the handle tightly, swing it back, and slam it against the wall.

You wrench it out, then lean forward to peer through the hole you made.

Turn to page 23.

-525603170:00

"I'll fix this!" you tell Kanisha and Other You, who has appeared in the doorway. You decide to crank the hand of the clock forward, the way it was.

"This should work," you say to Kanisha, who's now approaching. You hear the gears turning inside.

Then you see Kanisha reaching for the clock's hands.

"No!" you say. "Stop! You don't understand . . ."

There's suddenly somebody else in the reflection on the clock's glass front. It's an old, withered face. You gasp. The reflection mirrors your startled response.

"No," you say, realizing. You look down at your hands. They're pockmarked, with knobby knuckles and skeletal fingers. The face staring back at you looks ancient. Your eyes are sinking into their sockets. Your skin begins to droop down the side of your face.

The clock! Kanisha pushed the hands too far. Time spins as you drop to your knees.

You try to scream, but all you can do is wheeze. And when the clock chimes again . . .

You feel nothing but dust blowing into the night air.

THE END.

To try again, go back to page 93.

01:07

"Three!"

Kanisha's fingers open up and flatten into a sheet of paper.

Just like yours did.

"Hmm," she says. "That didn't work. Better try again."

"One . . ."

"Two . . ."

If you choose rock, turn to page 8.

If you choose scissors, turn to page 22.

11:46

You came here on a mission and you're going to see it through. Except there's an abundance of tombstones and very little time. Plus, once you find Avonlea's, you're going to need some kind of digging implement.

On cue, you step on an upturned shovel. The handle see-saws up and smacks you clean in the face. "Yee-ouch!" you spit.

The shovel falls back to the ground, and you bend down to retrieve it. That was convenient, if painful. It's like some unseen force WANTS you to dig up a grave. But which one? And is this force friend or foe?

You shake these uneasy thoughts from your mind. You've got to focus. You move swiftly, looking at the names: *LEWTON*, *DE PALMA*, until finally . . .

SMITHSON! Even better, the first initial is an A. But the rest of the name has eroded over time.

Hmm. It *could* be her grave. You could try digging here. But you can see the Smithson family name is on several other nearby tombstones.

If you dig up this grave, turn to page 117.
If you keep looking, turn to page 11.

12:53

With lightning-fast reflexes honed from years of playing video games, you snatch the book from Smithson. She whips her head in your direction, but you've already jumped back.

Maybe something in here can help. Didn't she mention spells? You start thumbing through the book, but you can't make heads or tails of the writing.

Then you spy a little envelope glued inside the back cover. A card with names and dates scrawled on it juts out of the envelope. You give it only a quick glance, because you suddenly hear a hissing sound.

Smithson has opened her mouth as if to speak, but instead of words, a long forked tongue rolls out. "I wasn't being entirely honest with you earlier," she hisses. Literally.

"Oh, crud," you say.

Smithson's tongue probes the room. Then her eyes roll back in their sockets, revealing glowing white orbs. Slowly, she rises from the chair, and you realize she's, like, seven feet tall and thin as a skeleton. Her frame is draped in a black shroud. She stalks towards you, arms outstretched. She takes a swipe and nearly gouges you with her claw-like hands.

"Ha! You missed!"

She opens her mouth wide and her tongue shoots farther out, wrapping around your leg and pulling you down as you drop the book.

Your back scrapes against the floorboards as Smithson drags you towards her. Her jaw, unhooking like a snake's, stretches impossibly large. You can see fanged teeth elongating as her eyes glow brighter. You detect a smile curving on her wide-open maw.

You're so close to her gaping jaws now. Close enough that she takes hold of your leg with her claws, pinning you down.

"Giiiiiive meeeeee my BOOOOOOOK!" Smithson screeches with a piercing cry that makes your ears ring.

The book! It might be your only advantage here. It's still lying on the ground close by.

You go to grab it, but it's just out of reach. You inch your fingers towards it. That card sticking out the back might be within your grasp—maybe you could use it to pull the book towards you. Or you could throw all your weight at the book and try to get a firmer grip.

If you stretch to reach the card, turn to page 97.

If you summon your strength to grab the book, turn to page 114.

22:23

Y ou can't decide if the voice is speaking out loud or if it's just in your head. Part of you wants to turn and run, but—

"*Come closer,*" the voice says.

You grit your teeth and edge nearer to the object. It's almost as tall as you are, and next to an old mirror. You can see your reflection loom large in the mirror as you move closer.

"*That's right. You're nearly there . . .*"

You try to shake the voice from your mind.

"*Just reach out. Pull the sheet off. You must. If you help me, I can help you . . .*"

Pulling the sheet off seems so easy. But that's what the voice wants you to do. Why? What's beneath it?

You reach a shaky hand forward. You're about to grab hold of the sheet and pull, but . . . wait . . .

If you pull the sheet off, turn to page 115.

If you get out of there, turn to page 125.

01:11

That book has power. If you can only understand it . . .

"Come on, hand that thing over," you say.

The man hesitates. "You are sure?"

"Sure I'm sure," you say.

"You are absolutely positive?"

"It's like you don't want me to have it."

"It is, isn't it? Very well," he says. "Sign here."

You write your name below the last one—Smithson.

Saying nothing, he slips the card back into the envelope and hands you the book. "Take care of it," he says.

"How long do I have it for? Two weeks? Three?"

"Indefinitely," he says with a smile.

You grow dizzy. Swaying back and forth, you try to steady yourself, but the room becomes a blur—

You're sitting. Rocking, back and forth. You stare into a fireplace. With an icy surge through your blood, you realize where you are.

You're in Smithson's chair. In the bricked-up room.

In your lap is the book. You scream, but the sound never leaves the room . . .

THE END.

To try again, go back to page 112.

01:52

"I'll do it," you tell your cousin.

Kanisha is still squinting at the writing scrawled in the margin. "Are you sure? It's so small, and this passage doesn't make any sense," she says.

But you can see it just fine. "Wait a second," you say. "*I'm* small now. And the writing is backwards. That's why I can read it. It's reflected perfectly."

"How convenient," Kanisha says.

"Yes, it does seem rather serendipitous," you muse.

You stare at the words inked in the margin. You're about to start reading when the book suddenly slips from Kanisha's grasp and lands with a heavy thud on the floor.

"Hey, careful with that. I'm trying to read," you say. "I don't want to mess up the spell."

Kanisha shrugs. "It just jumped out of my hands."

"Books don't jump, Kanisha."

She bends down to retrieve the book, holding your shard of mirror in her free hand. As she gets close to the book, the cover flips open and the pages start turning of their own accord—as if a strong wind has pushed through the house.

Only there is no wind.

The pages fan back and forth until the book separates into two clumps. Then it snaps open and closed repeatedly. Before Kanisha can pull her hand away, the book JUMPS up and CLAMPS DOWN on it.

Kanisha lets out a yelp.

She yanks her hand away, or at least she tries to, but the book is holding on tight. She tries again, only this time the world around you spins.

She's let the mirror go.

And you're flying right onto the—

Whump!

The force of the drop sends your shard of mirror sliding across the floorboards, right into a gap underneath the bookcase.

As the mirror skids to a halt, you find yourself staring through the narrow space between the floor and the bottom of the bookcase. Through a layer of cobwebs, you can see Kanisha struggling with the book. Only now, it's worked its way up her arm.

The book is eating her!

"Kanisha!" you cry out.

But she's too busy screaming and running around to do anything.

"KANISHA! I'M HERE! I'M HERE UNDER THE BOOKSHELF!" you scream at the top of your lungs. But she's too loud, and you're too small. You must sound like a mouse to her.

And then she runs out of view.

In the distance, you hear a door slam.

The house grows quiet.

"Kanisha . . . ?"

But there is no response. And the house is empty again, leaving you with no one but the spiders for company . . .

THE END.

To try again, go back to page 99.

01:11

"**N**ahhhh," you say. "You keep that thing."

"You have chosen . . . wisely."

BONG! You jump at the sudden noise from the old clock, then realize what it means.

"It's midnight," you say. "But the house! The ghosts! Kanisha!"

"I'm right here." You turn to see your cousin patting her chest and head like she's surprised to find them.

It hits you. "The book! It was the source of the hauntings," you say to the librarian. "Right?" He just smiles.

You narrow your eyes. "But if it's been in the house all this time, how did you even know about it?"

Who is this guy, anyway? Or, maybe the less you know, the better. "We're gonna fly."

"But . . ." Kanisha says. "I have so many questions . . ."

"You don't need all the answers." You grab her arm. As you step through the doorway, you realize you're in your local library. But you've never seen this man before. You wonder if he's even left that room in years . . .

00:00

You survived! There are ten other ways to escape the danger—try to find them all!

5256031456

"**L**ook!" you say, pointing just beyond where Avonlea's sitting. "It's Spider-Man!"

Smithson looks as confused as you'd hoped she would. She whips her head around, and you snatch her papers off the table.

"Aha! Gotcha!"

"I see neither spider nor man," she says, but you're already off and running towards the clock.

You've got this. As long as you don't do something silly, like trip over your untied shoelaces, you'll get to the clock in no time at all—

"Urf!" you shout, as your shoelaces catch in a knot of wood.

You slam down to the floorboards, hard. The papers spill from your fingers, sliding across the floor.

You get onto your hands and knees, stagger over to the pages, grab as many as you can, and make a break for the clock. You manage to get up and begin turning the hands clockwise to—

"Not so fast," Smithson says, placing a hand on you, but you can already feel the clock's abilities working, bringing you back to the future . . .

Turn to page 19.

05:26

mirror full of ghosts waiting for you? That's a lot to take in, and you have some questions. Starting with, "Were you the ones writing the messages on the door?"

"What messages?" one of the ghosts responds.

"Who are you talking to?" Kanisha pipes in. You wave her off.

"More importantly," says the ghost with no eyes, "only YOU can set us free."

A chill runs down your spine. "Set you free from this mirror?"

"From this house. She has trapped us here. And she is doing the same to you."

That's when you see a large, looming shadow reflected in the mirror. At first, you think it's just one of the ghosts crowded around you. But when you turn around, the woman from the painting is in the attic with Kanisha—sans painting.

"She wields too much power," one of the ghosts whispers. "Power from the book of spells."

"But only the book can stop her," says another.

"Okay," you say. "She wanted us to find it, but I ended up here in mirror, mirror on the wall land." You think for a second. Why did she come up here? Why

have the mirror transport you here in the first place? And how did she manage to get out of the painting without the book?

Kanisha suddenly whips around and lowers her video camera. "Who's there?"

The ghostly woman glides forward. "My name is Avonlea Smithson. I've met your friend, but not you . . ."

"Don't get close to her," you say loud enough to warn Kanisha. In return, she gives you a quick nod and ducks out of the way.

Avonlea tracks Kanisha's movement, but quickly focuses her attention on the mirror. "I see you have met the others."

"Let them go," you say flatly.

Avonlea throws her head back and lets out the kind of malicious cackle you only hear in bad horror movies. "You FOOL! How do you think they got into that mirror in the first place?"

You see Kanisha out of the corner of your eye. She's pointing to something. A trunk. She can see inside it, but you can't. She gestures to you, and you've been on camera with Kanisha enough to know what it means: STALL HER.

Turn to page 27.

08:40

RIGHT IS RIGHT! But there's so little around to catch your attention that you end up zoning out. Soon you don't know how long you've been trudging along. Maybe five minutes. Maybe more. So it's the smallest deviation from this monotony that catches your ear.

You hear faint voices. Gradually, as you take tentative steps forward, you see a group of people. Or, rather, you see THROUGH them!

These must be the ghosts who have been haunting the house. Your body goes into fight-or-flight mode, but as you crouch to run away, one of them points a bone-white finger in your direction.

"Oh, there you are. We've been waiting for you."

You look behind you to see if the ghosts are perhaps talking to someone else. But there is nobody there. "Who? Me?" you ask.

"Yes, you. Who else would we be waiting for?"

"Another ghost?"

"No ghost. Just you." The ghosts move closer.

"Is it really . . . ?" one of the ghosts—a small child—asks another ghost.

"Yes, it is. It's *the heir*."

You do a double take. "The what?"

"The heir, of course. To Smithson House."

You stand there, stupefied. The heir? When you finally open your mouth, the words spill out. "That's impossible. Smithson isn't my last name. There's nobody named Smithson in my family. You're wrong. You've got the wrong person!"

The ghost closest to you shakes his head and motions towards the cavern roof. "Only a *true* heir would see our messages. Only a *true* heir would be able to enter through the gateway Avonlea and Abraham Smithson opened all those years ago. Many others have tried. Tried and failed. And here you are, at last."

"But my parents—"

"Have likely never told you about your destiny. About what you must do. You would never believe it, and if you did, you would not want to try. That's why they had your cousin create that program. You were set up to follow her. To find us."

You try to swallow this story. It's unbelievable, and yet here you are in an impossible underground lair with these ghosts.

"Okay, let's assume I'm the heir. And that you've been waiting for me. What for?"

"Only the true heir will be able to open the doorway."

Man, they're really into this *true heir* stuff. You see there are not one but two doors built into the cavern wall behind them. They are completely identical.

"Is this the doorway I'm supposed to open? Which one?"

"Only the true heir will know . . ."

You turn back to the ghosts. "You've gotta be kidding me."

"One door will lead all of us to freedom."

"Sweet!" you say. Then you wrinkle your brow. "What about the other one?"

The ghosts lower their heads. "The other will bring about your imminent destruction."

You shake your arms angrily at the ghosts. "Who builds doors like this?"

"You must choose," the closest ghost says.

"I could turn back," you say.

You start to leave, and a huge boulder CRASHES down, blocking your way. You nearly jump into the river, but you catch yourself before toppling over.

Then you turn back to the ghosts. "Did you guys have anything to do with that?"

"Who, us?" the ghosts say.

You let out a long, weary sigh as you eye the two doors.

If you choose the door on the left, turn to page 109.

If you choose the door on the right, turn to page 129.

10:19

"**O**ver here!" you shout, waving your hands. You fight with all of your might to stay afloat. An icy grip pulls at your feet, dragging you down. You look into the inky black waters, and for a moment you think you spy something moving down there.

Ignoring whatever's pulling at you, you paddle like mad. You're nearly there—

You reach out and grab the edge of the boat, but the hooded figure doesn't move to help you. Whatever's under the water tightens its grip on your ankles and legs.

"Oh, no, you don't!" You give one hefty kick and free yourself. Then you heave your weight over the edge of the hull.

You did it! You blink. Why didn't that guy help you?

You prop yourself onto your elbows and look over to the tall hooded figure. He or she is silently paddling along the river, easily pushing against the current that nearly swept you away. How can that be?

"Uh, hey there," you say, trying to get this guy's attention. "Thanks for helping me out." Even you're not sure if you're being sarcastic.

You're about to say something else when the boatman slowly turns his head around.

Like, ALL THE WAY around.

The bones in his neck snap and crackle like they're breaking. You squeeze a gasp from your lungs.

Under the hood, you see not a face but a SKULL!

"You're most welcome," the skull says, as you scream.

"Yes, I often am greeted with such affections," the skeleton says.

You get up, looking for an escape. You want to jump back in the river, but now you can see what's under there. MORE SKELETONS. They're moving through the water like schools of fish.

You spin around. "Where am I?"

"This is the river of the dead," the skeleton says matter-of-factly. "If you're here, you have joined them."

"That's not true! I snuck in," you say.

"Very well. I am Charon. I escort souls to the underworld. You might as well sit back and enjoy the ride."

No way. You're not going down without a fight. But do you use your muscles or your words?

If you shove the boatman into the water, turn to page 96.
If you try talking him out of this, turn to page 105.

26:42

The clock is definitely bothering you the most.

For one thing, it's still keeping time. As you approach it you can hear a steady *tick, tick, tick.* Shouldn't it be an old relic like the rest of this place?

You spot fingerprints on the glass panel at the front of the clock. Ghosts don't have fingerprints, do they? You take a breath, then the panel suddenly swings open with a loud creak. Weird.

You peer inside. The clock's interior is so full of pendulums and gears it's like you're staring under the hood of an ancient automobile.

Tick. Tick. Tick.

The sound is louder now. It gets in your head, making you feel like time is somehow slowing down, like it doesn't even exist in this room ...

Heart in your throat, you breathe deeply. What if it does more than just tell time?

You look at the hands of the clock and wonder what would happen if you moved them. You decide to find out.

If you move the hands of the clock just a little, turn to page 10.
If you REALLY move the hands of the clock, turn to page 45.

06:44

You catch up with the zombie but decide to hold back so that you're not walking side by side. You still don't trust that this creature isn't going to turn around and bite you. But it's walking with purpose now, moving through the tombstones as if it's searching for one in particular.

You look at the names etched into the stones. You spot *Smithson* on some of them, but before you can tell the zombie to hold up so you can have a closer look, you nearly bump into the creature's bulk.

It's stopped right in front of one of the graves. It stands there, pointing a long, withered finger at it.

AVONLEA SMITHSON, the tombstone proclaims.

"Whoa!" you say. "You're substantially more helpful than I thought you would be."

The zombie turns to you and shrugs its shoulders. "Urghghrhg," it says. Then it points to something beside the tombstone. An old, rusted shovel.

"How convenient," you say suspiciously. As if the one grave you were sent to find and dig up has a shovel right beside it?

This is a little *too* convenient.

The zombie is still not making any move to eat you,

which goes against everything you've ever learned about zombies.

It stands there, shifting its weight from foot to foot.

"You want me to dig?" you say.

"Urghrhrhgh."

"Why don't you dig? You're the zombie."

Does it matter who digs? If you take the shovel, you'll have a weapon—a real weapon—in case things go sour.

On the other hand, that zombie has led you here. It might as well finish the job.

If you dig up the grave yourself, turn to page 65.

If you have the zombie dig up the grave, turn to page 133.

02:25

The only thing working in your favour is the element of surprise. "COWABUNGA, DUDE!" you roar.

"Wha—?" the boatman begins.

But you're already in action. You reach forward and grab hold of the heavy wooden paddle, then . . .

"TAKE THAT, SUCKER!" Your foot connects with the heavy cloak. You hear bones snap and—

The boatman is still standing. Pain surges through your body. Your scream echoes through the cavern.

You drop to the floor of the boat, clutching your leg that's now twisted out of shape.

A skeletal hand pushes through the robe and brushes your gangly leg. "Ouch," he says. "That's got to hurt."

You whimper.

"Don't fret, there will be plenty of time for this wound to heal. In fact, you have *all the time in the world.*"

You're certain he's smiling as he paddles down the river like your escape attempt never happened.

Everything around you grows darker as you move out of one world and into another.

THE END.
To try again, go back to page 24.

05:37

You manage to snag the card. But as you pull it towards you, it inches itself out, leaving the book behind . . .

As soon as that happens, your fingers start to tingle. Then your hand, and arm, and—

You look down to see your body vanishing. You try to let go of the card, but you can't move your hand. You can't even feel it. The whole room whirls around you until it's a dark blur, and then—

You're standing in a shadowy room. Bookshelves surround you, but this is not the bricked-up fireplace room. Smithson is nowhere to be seen, but the book is lying on the ground by your feet. It seems to be shimmering in the dim light.

You hear ticking in the background and spy a grandfather clock against a far wall. It's nearly midnight. Then someone clears their throat and you spin around. An old man is hunched over a large desk. He has thinning white hair and a face pockmarked with age. He does not look surprised to see you. He extends an arm and opens his hand as if expecting something.

"AHEM," he says.

"Who are you? Where am I?"

"The book, if you please."

You finally connect that this old dude wants the book you swiped from Smithson. You shrug and hand both the book and the card over to him. "You're not going to turn into a seven-foot-tall snake monster, are you?"

The man raises an eyebrow.

For some reason, this freaks you out more than Smithson's unhuman transformation.

He takes a look at the card, then slips it back inside its envelope.

He notices you're still staring at the book. "Yes?" he says.

"Is that card important?"

"It is a library book, and this card tells us who is in possession of the book."

"What, no barcode? That's old school . . ."

You think more about this as the man continues to examine the book. "That's a magic book, isn't it?" you ask.

He says nothing.

"A magic book that you can just . . . sign out of the library? Is that what this place is?"

The librarian eyes you carefully. "Do you truly wish to know the secrets of the book?"

If you say no, turn to page 84.

If you say yes, turn to page 80.

13:21

You don't land on the ground, but something breaks your fall. Where are you? You're not in the basement. There's slightly more light here, slanting in from a few windows in the roof.

The roof! An angled ceiling looms above you, which means you've somehow been transported to the attic. This makes no sense. There are piles of old, cobwebby boxes and bric-a-brac up here, including some dresses that flow in the breeze like delicate ghosts. It might not be as dank as the basement, but it's no less creepy.

You try to take a step forward, but your face knocks against something solid.

You put your hands out, and they are also blocked. It's like you've got a pane of glass separating you from the rest of the world. Like a . . .

"Mirror," you say, remembering you'd fallen into that basement mirror. You can see your reflection in a piece of glassware resting on a nearby shelf. It hits you—you're trapped in this mirror the same way that woman was trapped in the painting. "Aw, nuts!"

Maybe you can smash your way out. But with what?

You'd look around, but there's not really anywhere to look, exactly. Behind you is a reflection of the attic.

Only you can't move into the reflected world. You're trapped in a small sliver of existence between the glass and the reflection. It's confining and scary and you start to freak out. You kick at the glass, hoping to break it. Nothing. You stamp and scream and say a few swears that any reasonable publisher is not going to include in a children's book.

After your tirade, you lean against the glass and breathe heavily. What good did that do, except burn a few non-calories?

You hear the thump of approaching footsteps. You brace for action, wondering if the ghosts are on your tail.

A trap door opens in the floor. A shadow emerges into the attic. You get ready to scream and swear some more and then you see . . .

"Kanisha!" Your cousin has still got that video camera in her hands. She swings it around the attic, looking through the viewfinder.

"Kanisha, put that thing down!" you shout. Can she even hear you?

She calls your name. Phew!

"I'm right here," you say. You wave your hands and jump up and down. You see the moment she recognizes you in the mirror. Her hand trembles as she lowers the camera. Her eyes widen, and she shakes her head.

She turns around, looking for you.

"No, I'm here," you say. "IN THE MIRROR."

Slowly, she steps towards you. "How did that happen?"

"Ghosts," you tell her.

"Cool!" she says automatically. Then she thinks twice of it. "I mean, oh. Not good."

"I like the second answer better." You don't have a ton of time, and you think about how you can possibly get out of here. If the ghosts trapped Smithson in the painting, maybe you need to take her advice and find that book she was talking about. You quickly repeat her instructions to Kanisha.

But where is it? And how can you find it?

If you look for the book yourself, turn to page 13.

If you get Kanisha to look for it, turn to page 32.

04:43

"No thanks," you say to Abraham. "The sooner we get this over with, the sooner I can go home."

You reach down, pick up the shovel, and swing its rusted blade in the air. It gives a reassuring whoosh. "If she's as solid as you, I think this might do some damage."

Abraham jabs a finger at you. "Ha! You think a mere shovel could take on a Kandarian Ghoulite? In its natural state, that creature would break a shovel like a toothpick. After devouring you and I, of course. And it will squish us in its mouth like a pair of grapes. Oh, how you jest!"

Then Abraham disappears behind a tombstone.

"Seriously? You're running away?"

He emerges a moment later. He hoists what appears to be a MASSIVE BATTLE AXE and swings it through the air with an even mightier whoosh. It hits the tombstone and splits it in half.

You drop your shovel. "Oh, dang! Who are you? Conan the Barbarian? What else are you hiding behind random tombstones?"

Abraham is about to answer when—
SMASH!

You're thrown from your feet as a GIANT TEN-TACLE BURSTS OUT OF THE EARTH.

You land with a thud that tears your breath away as another tentacle erupts from the ground. Then another. And another. You frantically suck air back into your lungs as a slimy monster body gushes from a hole in the ground. The monster shifts form, staring at you with red eyes the size of softballs. It opens a maw full of jagged teeth the approximate size and shape of machetes. Also red. Probably bloodstained. You gulp.

"YOU FOOL!" the monster rages. "You've led me right to him!"

"Oh, I get it," you say. "That thing used me as live bait!"

One of the tentacles wraps around Abraham and hoists him off the ground. The battle axe falls to the muddy earth with a heavy thud.

Abraham squirms, but he's no match for the crea-ture. It retracts its tentacle so it's face to face with Abraham. Then it squeezes. "GIVE IT TO ME!"

"This ends NOW, you oozing mound of filth!" Abraham says. He reaches into his suit and pulls out an old piece of paper. It must be the missing page from Avonlea's book of incantations. "I will summon you back to the foul realm from which you pulled your fetid bulk!"

"YOU'LL SUMMON NOTHING BUT YOUR OWN DOOM!" the creature roar-laughs.

You stand there, trying to figure out how you can either get involved or get the heck away, but also impressed at the quality of the insults being hurled.

Abraham opens his mouth to read the incantation, but the creature snatches the paper from his hand with one of its free tentacles.

"YOU THINK YOU COULD OUTWIT ME? I AM INVINCIBLE!"

"And extremely loud," you say, trying to think. What if you go get the battle axe? Its metallic blade gleams in the moonlight. You don't need to kill this shape-shifting creature; you just need to injure it. Or better still, make it drop that page of spells. That will give you something to bargain with.

You grab the axe. It's super heavy in your hands. On second thought, maybe this won't be so easy. It's time to plan your attack.

If you whack the creature with the axe, turn to page 35.
If you hurl the axe at it, turn to page 42.

02:25

"**H**ey, you wanna make a deal?"

The boatman stops paddling and stares at you. "Huh?"

You've got his attention. Now what? "You heard me!" you bark, trying to sound like you've got a brilliant idea. "A deal. You let me go, and I'll . . . I'll get you spotlighted on *HAUNTS AND HOMES*!"

The boatman remains perfectly still.

Oh no. This is the worst idea you've ever had. You are as good as dead. You are on a one-way ticket to the underworld. You are—

"Do you KNOW Kanisha?"

Now it's your turn to stop in your tracks.

The boatman looks around. "She's not here, is she?"

"What?"

"Kanisha, the host of *Haunts and Homes*."

You nod your head. Slowly. "Yes?"

"I'm such a BIG FAN!" Charon says. He bends down so that his leering skull is right in your face. You fight the urge to back away. "Can you really get me on the show?"

"Totally," you say. "She's my cousin."

Charon throws his arms out. You think he's going

to rip you to pieces but instead he pulls you into a giant hug. "OMG!!!" he roars. "That is super-duper cool! I never get to be on any show. Mostly because the people I meet are already dead."

"Oh," you say.

"Yeah, it's a total bummer. They're all so sad, and, like, woe is me. I have a lot to say about the afterlife, and I think the living need to hear it. That way they can be better prepared when they drop into my realm."

You can't believe this is actually working. You also can't believe the gatekeeper to the underworld talks like a surfer from California, but you're going to go with it.

"So, how do we get out of here?" you say. "There's this house full of ghosts that are going to break into our world in just a few minutes, and—"

"Yeah, yeah. I'll take care of those guys," Charon says, waving you off. He turns and flashes what you can only imagine is a grin. "You just sit back and enjoy the ride. This is gonna be TOTALLY AWESOME!"

00:00

You survived! There are ten other ways to escape the danger—try to find them all!

09:29

o big *and* (you hope) go home! You grunt and heave, but manage to pull yourself onto the first branch. Thankfully the rest of the branches are spaced out so that you can manoeuvre through them like the rungs of a ladder. A ladder that scrapes and scratches at your skin, but at least you're making headway.

"Urgehghrhg!"

You stop and listen.

"Grrrrrghrnhh . . ."

That's not a good sound. For one thing, you tend to like voices with words attached.

You look down and see a DECREPIT ZOMBIE lumbering around the graveyard. Why *wouldn't* there be a zombie here? It's spotted you and is staggering towards the tree as only the undead can. Good thing you're already this high up, because the zombie doesn't appear to be able to do much except grunt.

You keep climbing. On the other side of the iron fence lies a thick blanket of trees and darkness. You can't see the world beyond it, but you're sure someone will help you find Kanisha if you can just get over there.

But the tree is too far away from the fence to jump from a standing position. You'll need to run the

length of the branch and make your best jump ever. If this were a video game, you'd just hit a button on the controller and get some solid hang time. But this isn't a video game. And those iron spikes look sharp.

"Urgh," you tell yourself.

"Urrrghghrhg," the zombie says. It seems to be looking from you to the fence. Does the zombie know something you don't?

But you're already up here. You might as well try.

You've got one shot at this. You train your eyes on the fence, ignoring the perilous drop to the ground and the hungry zombie waiting for food scraps, and you RUN!

The branch immediately bends under your weight. You keep running.

It's not going to work. It's not going to work—

You JUMP. You soar through the air.

"Ooooooooh," the zombie says.

"Whoa!" you say. The fence rushes at you. You might actually clear it! You're going to hit the ground hard, but maybe you'll be okay. You hurtle towards the darkness on the other side and—

Turn to page 41.

03:56

"I took the right path to get here; maybe the left door will lead us back."

"That rings of solid logic!" the ghost closest to you says.

You wrap your fingers around the handle and pull. The door is heavy, and you have to put all of your muscle into it. It scrapes against the stone floor as it opens, then you step into a dark room. Your footsteps echo, suggesting a vast space inside. The ghosts follow you in.

"So far, so good," you say, mostly to keep from scaring yourself.

The door slams shut. You are trapped. You try to feel around for the handle, but you find nothing. "Still good," you say, although your voice is beginning to waver. "It's a good thing I'm the true heir . . ."

One of the ghosts stifles a laugh.

"What?"

"Well, we were just kidding about the whole *true heir* business," the ghost says.

"Huh?"

"It's one of our hilarious jokes."

"It's how we amuse ourselves," another chimes in.

This isn't good. You fumble your way through the dark, looking for anything that could help you. But all you can see are the illuminated faces of the ghosts around you.

Soon those faces illuminate other things.

Big, long, white things. The room is full of them. You can see them now—in the walls, above you on the ceiling. They glow in the dark, and they all end in sharp points. Some of them have red stains.

The room is full of GIANT FANGS.

"Let me out!" you cry.

"But we need to feed our pet," one ghost says.

"Our pet is so very hungry," says another.

The walls begin to close in on you, the teeth moving closer and closer, and—

CRUNCH.

THE END.

To try again, go back to page 24.

09:29

You climb on top of a tombstone near the fence. You're going to have to jump, grab hold of the bars, and work your way over, but it's better than a risky leap from a tree. You crouch, eyeing the bars. Three. Two. One . . .

SOMETHING GRABS YOUR LEG! "EEEEARRGH!" you scream.

"URRGGHGH!" a voice screams back.

You look down. A hand with pallid, putrefying flesh is clamped around your ankle. You are assaulted by the rank stench of death and have to hold back throwing up as you take in the HORRID ZOMBIE holding your leg.

"Yeaaargh!" you shout.

"Urrghghrhghrrr," it says. Bugs are crawling through its teeth and flapping black tongue.

Instinctively, you kick. This throws the zombie backwards, freeing you from its grasp, but also pitches you off the top of the tombstone and into the mud. *SPLAT!*

You get up, heaving air into your lungs.

The zombie looks dazed as it moves incessantly towards you. This creature won't give up easily. You get into fight-or-flight mode. What's it going to be?

If you take off, turn to page 25.

If you face off, turn to page 33.

14:03

"Yes," she says impatiently. "I'm a ghost."

"Like, a *dead* ghost?"

"What other kind are there?"

"I hear you. But what are you doing in this room? It looks like someone trapped you here."

Smithson holds up an old leather-bound book. "It's because of this," she says. "I wrote it. I did not realize that the spells I collected would summon such terrible forces into our world. And now they've trapped me here. Only you can help me."

"Why me?"

She flips through the book. "This tome is incomplete. I need you to bring me the final page."

"Oh. That shouldn't be a problem. It must be here somewhere. I'll grab it for you."

"The missing page is in the graveyard behind the house—"

"Weird, but okay."

"—*buried* with me," she finishes.

You make a face. "On second thought . . ."

Smithson gives you an urgent glance. "You cannot escape the house on your own. The spirits have seen to that. The only way out of its walls is through there."

She points to the fireplace.

"Hang on a second. You want me to step *into* the fire? Are you nuts?"

"The fireplace is not a fireplace. It is, in actuality, a portal that will transport you to the graveyard."

"Looks more like a portal to getting third-degree burns."

"You need to trust me."

You look from Smithson to the fire, then back to Smithson again. Trust her? She's a strange ghost woman bricked up in this room. What if she's behind all of the horrible things going on in this house? Maybe someone should take that weird book away from her.

You could get Kanisha for help, but who even knows where she is. Plus, you realize as you look at your phone's clock, time's running out. You need to make a move. Now.

If you go through the fireplace, turn to page 3.

If you grab the book out of Avonlea Smithson's hands, turn to page 77.

05:37

You muster every ounce of strength you have and dive towards the book with Smithson still holding on to your legs—

Got it!

"You want your book? Take it!" you shout, hurling it with all your might at this banshee-like monster.

The book soars through the air. It's a hardcover tome that could do some serious damage. This is your chance to escape!

Then the book bounces off Smithson's head like it's a Nerf dart. You both watch it slam against the floor.

"Seriously?" you say.

Smithson tightens her grip on your legs and pulls you closer and closer to her giant mouth. It's like looking into the jaws of a great white shark. Her teeth, you note, are just as sharp. "Look who's tongue-tied now," she hisses.

You claw desperately at the floor to get away, but your fingernails can only scratch marks into the floorboards as you are slowly pulled into Smithson's waiting gullet.

THE END.

To try again, go back to page 112.

21:31

Oh, what the heck! Off goes the sheet.

You're staring at a life-sized portrait of a woman wearing a long dress that looks like it was in fashion over a hundred years ago. She has a pained expression on her face, like she wasn't happy to have her portrait made.

And then she blinks. You gasp. No. It couldn't be.

Then the woman in the painting turns her head to stare you right in the eyes, and you do the only sensible thing you can do.

You scream your face off.

The woman clamps her hands over her ears as you scream some more. Then, when you're out of breath, she clears her throat. "Finished?"

"Wh—" you sputter. "What? How?"

"Yes, you don't seem like the kind of person who communes with spirits from beyond your astral plane regularly, do you?"

You blink. You keep thinking she's going to grow fangs, jump out of the painting, and bite your head off, but maybe she's not that kind of ghost. Maybe you've been watching too many horror movies.

"Were you the one writing those messages on the door?" you ask.

She rolls her eyes. "Do I look like the kind of spirit who wants to get their clothes dirty?"

You shrug. "Who are you, then?"

She points to a bronze nameplate screwed into the frame.

"Avonlea Smithson?" you say, looking back up at her.

She nods. "The one and only."

"But that means . . . this is your house!" You stop and think about this. "Wait, why is your picture in the basement? Shouldn't it be upstairs on the wall or something?"

"Yes, it should be. But I'm trapped. Not just in this basement, but in this painting. There are other spirits at work in this dwelling."

Like the ones who scrawled that bloody message on the door.

"Yeah, I know," you say. "They say they're going to break into our world in like . . . twenty minutes," you mention, checking the clock on your phone.

"Then we don't have much time," Smithson says. "Listen closely. You must do exactly what I say if you want to escape this house alive."

Turn to page 14.

10:28

Time is of the essence, so you jam the shovel into the earth and dig. And dig. And *dig*. And after you've dug a good-sized hole, guess what?

You dig some more.

If anything, this adventure has given you a newfound appreciation for the hard and often under-valued work of society's gravediggers.

These are the thoughts that swim through your mind as you complete this monotonous task, until your shovel finally connects with something hard and wooden.

"Bingo!" you say, sweat dripping down your brow. "Almost there." With the next scoop of your shovel, you clear a section of dirt from the casket.

There's something on top of the casket—a plaque. It's caked with mud, so you have to get down on your hands and knees to wipe it clean. Maybe there's an important message on it?

You peer at the letters on the plaque. It's not a message. Not a memorial.

It's a name.

YOUR NAME.

You stand up. "That's impossible—"

"No," a voice calls from above. You look up. A flash of lightning silhouettes a skeletal figure standing on the ground overhead. A clap of thunder follows, or is that your own heart thudding in terror?

"Mrs. Smithson!" you cry out.

"I'm so pleased you managed to find that well-placed shovel. And this grave."

"But the tombstone says *Smithson*," you say weakly.

"Exactly," Avonlea Smithson says. "I feel confident no one will go looking for you here."

"But you said you needed my help . . ."

"You did help," she coos. "You wasted enough time to get us to midnight. Didn't you read the message I put on the wall when you came into my home? Now I can take your body—and break through to your world."

You shake your head. No, no, no . . .

Avonlea doesn't say anything else. She just grins. There's something about her smile that sets you off. It's too wide, her lips stretched just a bit too far apart for any normal mouth. She licks them, like she's about to enjoy a large meal.

THE END.
To try again, go back to page 3.

5256031456

"Look," you say. "I didn't mean to trespass. I'm actually from the future."

She waves you off. "Balderdash," she says. "That's impossible."

"Oh, is it?" You reach into your pocket and pull out your cellphone. You don't get any reception in the past, but you do have a bunch of photos on your phone.

"Check this out." You hold the device up and start swiping through your selfies.

She takes the phone from your hand. "Incredible," she says. Then she pokes at the screen. Instantly the room is full of the heavy metal music you'd downloaded the day before.

Smithson drops the phone and stares at it in horror. "What. Is. That?!"

"Oh, just my tunes," you say. "Future tunes." You pick up the phone and switch the sound off.

The look on her face has changed. "Are you one of the phantoms?" she asks.

You bang on the table. "Can phantoms do *that*?"

"I have studied the ways of poltergeists. They can indeed move objects and make noises."

"Ms. Smithson, I'm totally real. I come from the

future. A future where there are ghosts in your house."

"There is a ghost in my house right now . . ." she says.

"Not me. I'm real. I'm talking about the evil spirits that are about to break into our world, all because of your book. Do you really want that?"

Smithson looks down at the papers she's been writing on. A smile creeps across her face. "Oh, thank you, kind spirit. You have given me an idea."

"Oh no," you say. You begin to realize what is happening.

"I'd merely wished to communicate with spirits. But now I see they can be *summoned* as well." She gets to her feet and begins to walk away, lost in thought.

"Whoa, hold up there, lady! You don't understand. They're going to haunt this house!"

But she's not listening to you anymore. Great. Just great. *You're* the one who caused all of this in the first place!

THE END.

To try again, go back to page 93.

05:26

The ghosts push towards you, but you pretend they're not there. "You'd better find that book, and fast!" you shout to Kanisha.

"Oh, but there's nowhere to go. No way out," the eyeless ghost says.

The other ghosts move in closer. "We have been waiting for a fresh body. One who can still emerge from the mirror."

But before you can process what they're saying, the eyeless ghost presses himself RIGHT INTO YOU. You feel a shiver through your entire body.

There is a brief pause, then the ghost closest to you asks, "Did it work?"

Your mouth opens of its own accord, and a raspy voice lets out a long, sustained "Yesssssssss."

You clamp a hand over your mouth, but a force takes over, moving your hand away. You try to shake your head, try to call out, but you are locked in place.

Kanisha stares at you in the mirror. "What are you doing?"

The other ghosts move towards you, one after the other. Your body is wracked with shivers, one for each ghost. You go numb. You are turning towards Kanisha, but it's not you moving your body. It's not YOU placing your hands against the glass of the mirror.

The ghosts are inhabiting your body. They've seized control of you, and they twist your mouth into a cruel, wicked smile.

Kanisha doesn't understand, but she will soon.

A dark shadow has entered the attic.

It looms closer, and you know who it is. It's Avonlea Smithson—the woman from the painting. This was all part of her trap. She's not holding these ghosts prisoner. She's using you to set them free . . .

You try to open your mouth to warn Kanisha, but before you can wrestle with the power of these ghosts, you see Avonlea—free of the painting—drift into Kanisha's body. Kanisha shivers. Her eyes roll back in her head, and when she opens them again and looks at you, you can tell Kanisha's not in control of her body anymore.

"At last," Avonlea says, through Kanisha's mouth, "we are free . . ."

THE END.

To try again, go back to page 99.

14:17

"I'll be right back," you say. "I'm going to check the bookshelf upstairs."

"Hurry," Smithson says. "You don't have much time."

Taking the old lantern, you turn and run up the staircase, back to the main floor.

Kanisha is still nowhere to be found. You get a sinking feeling the ghouls in this house have her and that they're after you now. Your heart thumps wildly in your chest as you move through the house and the lantern's light throws eerie elongated shadows that stretch across the floor like angry vipers.

You ignore them, you ignore the creaking of the floorboards, and you even ignore the sounds at the periphery of your hearing. Sounds like squeaking and cackling that set your teeth on edge.

You stop when you get to the bookshelf. There are so many books here, and so little time.

You think. What did Smithson say? That the book of incantations was an old leather-bound book? You look at the shelves full of dusty old books and balk. They're ALL old leather-bound books!

"Gah!" you blurt.

Some of the books have foil lettering stamped on their spines, so you're able to glean a bit more about them. But they're all just books about history, and boring encyclopedias, and ledgers of old expenses, and spirit guides, and—

You look back at that last spine. "Whoa!"

"*Tobin's Spirit Guide*," you say aloud. You blink and double-check that you're not misreading the spine. "That sounds about right."

But hang on. *Is* this the right book? If it were, wouldn't Avonlea have said to find this specific one?

You step back to get a better look at the entire bookshelf.

You search it carefully, scanning each row, looking for a book that doesn't quite fit.

There! Right on the top shelf! There's a book that's not pushed in all the way, and without any dust covering it. Somebody . . . or something . . . has moved that book recently. They or it put it up nice and high, almost out of view. You wouldn't even have noticed it if you hadn't stepped back to search.

Which book should you check first?

If you choose *Tobin's Spirit Guide,* turn to page 29.
If you choose the book on the top shelf, turn to page 67.

21:31

It's a trick. Gotta be. You step away from the object.

"Don't even think about it!"

The voice is so loud you clutch your ears. The lantern clatters to the ground, making the shadows writhe, and—

The sheet around the object flies off, revealing a painting underneath. It's a large portrait of a woman, her face contorted into an expression of hideous excitement. You want to think it was just a draft, and not that this painting is actually haunted, but now the sheet is sailing through the air towards you.

You run several steps, but you trip over something and fall to the ground with a heavy thud. You look over to see a toppled box of junk. It's just some old tools, and a knife, and—

The sheet is billowing so close and so quickly that you can't see anything else. You've got to throw the knife and hope you can tear right through this haunted piece of canvas.

"You had your chance. Now you'll pay!"

"Oh, sheet!" you yelp.

Turn to page 5 . . .

. . . or page 36.

22:23

Y ou look over the hole in the ground. There's a sizeable pile of earth in front of it. A shovel lies to the
side. What was Kanisha doing here? More to the point,
how could she have dug a hole like this so quickly?
Unless . . . it was already there to begin with.

You get on your hands and knees and pull some of
the cold, wet earth from the hole. It smells like something's died in it.

As you move your hands across the hole again, you
feel something—something solid. You knock on it, and
it makes a hollow sound.

A trap door, perhaps? You feel for the handle, then
wrap your fingers around it. You have to pull so hard to
open it, you end up half-falling into the hole.

Immediately, you sense that something is wrong.
"Kanisha?" you call out, and your voice echoes down
below. Where does this door even lead?

You put your head through the opening to get a
better look, but you slip and lose your balance.

Now you're falling.

Turn to page 24.

06:17

You get Kanisha to walk you out of the attic and down two flights of stairs to the main floor. You remember seeing a huge bookcase when you came in. If there's one place you can find an old leather-bound book, it'll be here.

The problem: all of the books look old and leather-bound and you've still got a needle-in-a-haystack challenge.

"Where do we even start?" Kanisha wonders aloud.

You think. "She said it was leather-bound . . ."

"Yeah, they're ALL leather-bound. Urgh. And covered with dust."

You scan the shelves. Darn it, they all look like old books. All old, all boring, all . . .

You blink.

You can feel a throbbing in your temple. You look at the books on the bottom shelf. The throbbing goes away. You crane your neck up, and as your eyes pass one of the books, your head starts to spin. You blink and stare at the book that's making you dizzy.

"Try that one," you tell her.

While holding the mirror in one hand, Kanisha

reaches up and pulls the old book off the shelf. She thumbs through its pages.

Soon enough, she stops at one page, jabbing her finger at an instruction. "Hey, nice going. This must be it," she says.

"Really? Why?"

"For one thing, there's a bookmark right here," Kanisha says, pulling out a faded yellow strip of paper. "Plus, somebody wrote a note in the margin. I think it says, '*Incantus Iniquitous*. Read this passage to raise the dead.'"

You nod. "Works for me. One of us needs to read that passage, and fast!"

If you read the passage, turn to page 81.
If you let Kanisha read it, turn to page 51.

If you read the passage, turn to page 81.
If you let Kanisha read it, turn to page 51.

03:56

You clasp the handle of the door on the right and pull. It opens easily enough, and as you pass through the threshold you realize where you are: back in the main foyer of Smithson House.

This is weird. "Why bring me back here?" you ask the ghosts.

"For me," a familiar voice says. And your cousin doesn't seem the least bit surprised to find a bunch of ghosts hovering around you.

"Great!" you chirp. "We can get out of here if we help these ghosts with something."

"About that . . ." Kanisha says.

"Look," a ghost says, and points to a portrait on the wall that you completely overlooked earlier.

There's something familiar about the person it depicts. You wipe away some cobwebs and gasp—it's KANISHA! "Impossible," you say. You turn to your cousin.

"Well, I had to bring you here somehow," she says. "We need to determine the next heir, you see."

"I don't."

Kanisha motions to the house. "This is more than just a house. It's a gateway to the world beyond life itself. Members of our family have been its heirs for

generations." She moves past you and brushes cobwebs away from another portrait. You gasp again, because this time IT'S A PICTURE OF YOU!

Speechless, you stagger away from Kanisha and towards the relative safety of the ghosts.

Kanisha speaks for you. "You want to know what this means, don't you?"

But you're still staring at the portrait. It's an old painting. But it's you. You're wearing old-fashioned clothing. How can this be?

"Our family line has very interesting traditions. We vie for control of the house. And whoever wins control of the house also controls the gateway."

"So what do we do?" you ask. "Fight to the death or something? C'mon, Kanisha, we're not like that."

But Kanisha just holds out her fist. "Are you ready?"

You shrug. "Beats killing one another."

She nods, then says, "The house will consume the loser anyway."

Oh man. These aren't good odds, but what else can you do? You hold your fist across from hers.

"On three," she says.

"One . . ."

"Two . . ."

If you choose rock, turn to page 8.

If you choose paper, turn to page 75.

If you choose scissors, turn to page 22.

08:40

LEFT IS BEST! Left is also incredibly boring. Step after step, you trudge onward. Are you going to get out of here by midnight? Is there any way to save Kanisha? Or yourself? You lower your head, thoughts racing through your mind—

WHUMP!

You land face first in the dirt, then look up and see stairs.

That's right—a stone staircase is cut into the cavern wall. It zigzags in little switchbacks, leading up into the darkness.

"No way!" And with that, you're back on your feet, racing upwards. It's amazing how much energy you still have after taking that pounding against the rocks, then walking along the riverbank forever. You take the stairs two at a time, easily pivoting at the switchbacks.

You reach a point where the light seems to diminish, so you get on your hands and knees to feel your way around. Then your head bangs against something hard.

The roof of the cave? No, it can't be. This staircase has to have a purpose.

You feel around above your head, and your hands knock against something wooden. A trap door? Ha!

Does it lead to the basement? Is this the same one you fell from?

You find a knot in the wood and pull the door towards you. Dirt rains down on your face. You don't even care. This is the way out!

You reach a hand up. The dirt feels different here. It's cold and wet and full of leaves and roots.

You thrust your other hand up and feel solid ground. You splay your arms out and pull the rest of your body up. You drag yourself onto the ground, panting. You did it!

Only, wait.

You look down at your arm. In its place is just a set of long bones. It must be some kind of illusion, but your other arm is the same.

You pull them towards your face, bones jiggling and flexing.

"No!" you scream. You're not in the basement. You're in a graveyard. Tombstones surround you.

"This is impossible," you whimper.

Then you turn around. You see you've sprung out of a freshly dug grave. But the old, weathered tombstone in front of the grave looks like it's always been there.

On it, a name. Yours . . .

THE END.

To try again, go back to page 24.

05:59

"Here, you dig," you say, handing the shovel to the zombie. "You know what's going on here more than I do anyway."

The zombie looks at you and grunts. Then it takes the shovel and gets to work.

You watch as the animated cadaver sinks the shovel's blade into the earth and pulls out large clumps. It's making quick work of a job that would have taken you a long time.

The small pile beside the grave quickly turns into a large mound as the zombie descends deeper and deeper into the hole. Finally, the shovel hits something hard.

Carefully, you peer into the freshly dug hole. The zombie is standing on the exposed surface of an old wooden casket. It motions to you excitedly.

You still don't trust that zombie. "Pass me the shovel," you say.

"Grurughr," the zombie responds, handing you the shovel. You slide down the side of the hole, holding the shovel tightly in case the zombie tries any funny business.

Then the zombie bends down and PUNCHES A HOLE in the casket.

"Yee-ouch!" you say.

"Urrrrrrgh," the zombie grunts, almost smiling.

It rummages a hand around inside the casket. Then it gives an excited grunt and pulls something out.

You back away, tightening your grip on the shovel.

"Urrghrhh! Urrghrhg!" the zombie says, and you see what it's holding.

"No way," you gasp. It's the page Smithson said she had been buried with.

You eye the zombie. How did it know that's what you were after? And why is it reading through it like that?

"Urrghrhg!" the zombie says again, jabbing a gory finger at the page.

Carefully, slowly, you reach your hand out and take it. You stare quizzically at the page. "Spell for Undoing Death's Curse," you read aloud.

The zombie nods excitedly.

"Oh well." You shrug. "Here goes nothing." You read the passage: "Oh, Gobthulk the mighty! Hear my cries! Reverse the curse! Send forth the power of Oooglethrump with great speed!"

You shake your head. "Well, that's just a load of horse dung," you say.

CRACK!

You jump as a flash of lightning hits the tombstone above you. There's a huge clap of thunder, and another flash in the same spot.

You drop the shovel—you don't want to get fried by lightning.

Another bolt zaps down, right into the grave! The zombie blazes with white hot light.

"URRRRRRRGH!"

You try to scramble away, but there's nowhere to go. Thunder rolls as the zombie goes into spasms. And then . . .

"URRHGHRHG . . . HUMBLE THANKS, KIND SIR!"

You shake your head. "Hey, what?"

The zombie licks what's left of its lips with its blackened tongue. It creaks its head from side to side. "Oh, what a bother these last years have been. I am eternally grateful for what you have done, in every sense of the word."

"You . . . you can talk!" you say.

The zombie regards you and smiles. "Of course I can talk. I have several degrees in philosophy, English literature . . ."

"But you're dead. You were grunting and moaning, and . . ."

"Oh, that. It was the curse, you see. Smithson did not know what powers she had unleashed with that book. I assisted her in compiling it," the zombie says, in a genteel voice. "My curse was to wander this graveyard, waiting for someone to find the portal. For someone to lift the curse. I did not expect a child."

"I'm not a child."

"Forgive me. A young adult, perhaps?"

"Yeah, that's more like it."

You notice the zombie is starting to lose its form. You can see right through it. Right to the other side of the grave. The zombie notices this as well. "Oh, it's happening quicker than I thought."

"What is?"

"The undead. We are leaving. When you climb out of the grave, you will find that you can retrace your steps back to the house. To find your cousin, no doubt."

"How did you know about Kanisha?"

"Oh, you mere mortal. The living never understand the complexities of this universe. At least, not while there is breath in your body."

And with that, the zombie evaporates into thin air, leaving you slack-jawed and holding Smithson's missing page.

Who knows if what the zombie said is true. But there's only one way to find out. You pocket the paper and make your way out of the grave. Hopefully you don't wind up in another one for a long, long time.

00:00

You survived! There are ten other ways to escape the danger—try to find them all!

02:29

"**K**anisha, I'm coming!" you say. "Just keep calling to me. I can barely see in here!"

You wave your phone's flashlight, desperately searching through the darkness for any sign of your cousin.

"Closer," she says. "You're almost here."

You step towards the voice, but then you hear her again. "No, colder. Really cold." You step in the other direction. "That's right. Warmer. You're getting warmer."

You can't believe you're playing a game of hot or cold right now, but it seems to be working.

"Yes!" she says. "You're super hot. Keep coming this way."

You strain to see through the inky blackness as the light begins to fade. The flashlight is sucking the power from your phone's battery. Even if you do find Kanisha, how are you going to find your way out of this room in the dark? You're not sure you can make it back to that swinging bookshelf on your own. But maybe Kanisha knows another way out.

"Kanisha, can you hear me?"

"Better than that!" she says, her voice brightening. "I can see you. You're almost there."

You shake your head. "I can't see anything," you start, but then after another step you notice something.

A form, a few steps ahead. The light is dimming, but you can make out Kanisha's familiar outline. She's sitting on the floor, her knees hugged to her chest, rocking back and forth. Her hair has fallen over her face so you can't see her eyes or facial features. You can't tell where exactly in the room you are, but at least you've found your cousin.

You quickly move closer, until you're standing over her. You reach a hand out to help her up. "It's me," you say.

But she just keeps rocking back and forth.

You bend down so that you're at her level.

"Kanisha?"

But now she's not saying anything. She's just making little sobbing noises, like she's crying, or . . . laughing?

"Kanisha, what's going on? I'm here. I found you. Let's get out of here."

"You found me," she repeats, modulating her voice so it kind of sounds like yours.

"Yeah, I know. We can go home now."

"But we *are* home," she says, and she starts to make that weird sobbing sound again.

You shake your head. "Kanisha, are you okay?"

Just then she stretches out, and you see that the person in front of you is dressed like Kanisha, and

looks like Kanisha, right down to the same hair, same skin and even the same face.

Almost.

Because there are also opaque red orbs where her eyes should be. They seem to stare right through you.

And when she opens her mouth to speak, you see little rows of sharp, sharp teeth, then you smell her breath and you gag. You've never smelled anything so foul!

You stumble onto your butt. You try to back away, quickly, but she's already leapt towards you. She scuttles forward like a crab, and the last thing you see before your cellphone dies is that face.

Then you're back in darkness.

You feel her hands clamp over your arms, pulling you towards her.

You hear that weird sobbing sound.

And you—

THE END.

To try again, go back to page 14.